TO KILL A CATFISH

Polly Harris

PAULINE HARRIS
Editorial

This book is a work of fiction. Any references to real events, places, or people are used fictitiously. Other names, events, characters, or places are a product of the author's imagination and any resemblance to actual names, events, people, or places is completely coincidental.

© 2022 by Polly Harris.

Printed in the United States. All rights reserved. Unauthorized reproduction of this book in any form is prohibited. For information, contact Pauline Harris Editorial.

Paulineharriseditorial.com
Editing by: Pikko's House
Cover Design by: Mitxeran

ISBN: 9798446494507

For all the girls who've dated douchebags – don't worry, karma's a bitch.

Chapter 1

The funny thing about cheaters is that if they've done it once, they're bound to do it again. I didn't use to think that—second chances and all—but now I know it to be true. Nobody really wants to believe it, though. We assume others are like us—caring, loving, loyal. So, we tend to give people more chances than they deserve.

Until you find out they've cheated on you, not once, but throughout the entirety of your relationship, and you feel like smacking their head into a brick wall. Or catching them red-handed.

```
Sarah: That's hot. I like
smart guys.
Justin: 😊
```

For the record, Justin is not that smart. His Instagram profile is a douchey picture of himself on a motorcycle that I'll bet isn't his. He has John Lennon sunglasses on and isn't smiling. Besides, our entire conversation has been less than intellectually stimulating.

I wonder why this girl even likes him. Jaclyn is her name. Jaclyn who, like many girls before her, reached out asking if I'd bait Justin into "cheating." She's had her suspicions. They've been dating for almost a year. She caught him once, and he swore he'd never do it again, but I'm about to prove him wrong in three . . .

Two . . .
One . . .

```
Justin: You should come over.
```

Well, there you go.

```
Sarah: You're single, right?
Justin: Yeah.
```

Didn't take him long to respond to that one. I screenshot the messages, along with a few more above it. Poor Jaclyn. Poor Justin, too, I suppose, but serves him right for chatting up an Instagram blonde way out of his league. She's way too hot for him. And too good for him. Too good for anyone, really.

Brooklyn is perfection. The girl everyone wants to be. She literally models for fun on the side. She's also, like, the nicest person on the planet. Nothing like me. God, I don't even know how we became friends. We're polar opposites in all ways possible. She's tall and blonde, I'm short with black hair. She's a giant ray of
 sunshine and I'm . . . honestly kind of a bitch.

And that's how we snag lovely catches just like Justin. With Brooklyn's smile and my complete disdain for men's feelings, it's a pretty great setup. They fall for her looks and my charm, and then I sucker punch them in the balls by sending dozens of screenshots right to their girlfriends.

Like I'm doing now.

I send the array of screenshots and wait. I see the delivered sign and the notice that she's read it. It usually takes them a minute to process. I can't imagine it's a great feeling. Knowing your boyfriend lied about being single and was about to go hang out with some random girl.

I see the three little dots dancing above the text screen. Then they go away. I sigh, chucking my phone onto the couch cushions. I feel bad, but only slightly. I've been doing this long enough that the guilt only lasts a heartbeat, and it's quickly replaced by something else. Vindication. Because Jaclyn is going to move on from Justin. She's not going to spend another year of her life shackled to this asshole who's cheated on her with who knows how many women. It sucks now, but she'll be better for it. Just like I was.

My phone buzzes and I pick it back up.

```
Jaclyn: Thanks.
```

I bite my lip. It's easier when they're mad. When they call him names, when they vent, even when they fight with me. *You're lying. This isn't true.*

Somehow those screenshots are fake. By her answer, I think Jaclyn knew it was true. She's not surprised. Or even angry. Just sad.

Ugh. Normally, I cut contact after this, but I pull up Justin's Instagram profile, glare at his stupid fucking picture one last time, and send him a message.

```
Sarah: You're an asshole.
```

Chapter 2

I can see the bonfire in the distance, a glowing orange orb in a field of night. Brooklyn parks her car in the long line of others scattered throughout the hastily mowed field, and we jump out.

There is a line of trucks circling the fire, tailgates down with drinks and red solo cups littered about. It's way past sunset in this small farming town in Idaho—the town whose population is owed mainly to the college students who flock in and out seasonally. Away from the main stretch of town, there's nothing to see for miles around but darkness. Darkness and a large, raging bonfire.

"This is actually quite the turnout," Brooklyn mutters as we approach. "I thought more kids would've gone home by now."

It's early June, meaning school's been out for a week or so. Enough time has passed that the town of Ozona has dwindled in size, and the only remaining college kids are upperclassmen who live off campus and rent year-round. Like me and Brooklyn. Like most of the kids here.

I see someone toss a large pile of dried-up hay—probably gathered from the ground nearby—into the fire, glowing dark red as it crackles and melts.

"Brooklyn!" someone shouts and rushes out at us from the darkness. Brooklyn is immediately engulfed in a hug, her long blonde locks waving as she's jolted backward.

She laughs. "Hey, Sylvie."

"So glad you made it," Sylvie says, releasing her. "Did you hear about Kinsey's reading list for next semester? It's insane." Brooklyn and Sylvie are in the same major and share most classes.

Brooklyn groans. "I'm too afraid to look."

Sylvie glances over at me. "Hey, Vally."

I shoot her a grin. The typical interaction. Everyone navigates toward the bubbly Brooklyn, and then a few minutes later, they notice me. The standoffish one who doesn't say much. I don't really mind. It's kind of nice. Brooklyn's almost like a shield. Taking the brunt of whatever social encounter we end up stumbling into. And I know she loves it, so it's basically a perfect symbiotic relationship. Or is it parasitic? I suppose symbiotic only applies to mutual benefits. Honestly, I'd say Brooklyn gets a good deal too. After I chewed out some bitch freshman year who called Brooklyn a slut, people know not to mess with her.

We were assigned roommates in the dorms and met our first day on campus. At first, I honestly had my doubts. What could I possibly have in common with a chatty, supermodel-esque cheerleader? My hobbies include video games and listening to depressing music. But after fifteen days of Brooklyn smiling at me nonstop, bringing me lattes, and generally just being the most nauseatingly nice person ever, I caved. And we've been weirdly inseparable ever since.

Don't get me wrong: Brooklyn has other friends. Like Sylvie. But she mostly hangs out with me. I think she likes how I sarcastically shoot down all her ideas while she forces me to tag along anyway. Like tonight.

"Do you guys want beers?" Sylvie asks.

"Yeah," Brooklyn says.

"Sure," I add.

She leads us over to the nearest truck with a keg of something precariously balanced on the tailgate. She grabs some suspicious-looking solo cups. Are they used? They were kind of just sitting there. Not in their nice little stack like they come in, but just . . . there.

I bite my lip and take the offered drink. Whatever. If I get some disgusting virus, I'll just blame Brooklyn, and it'll give me fuel to tease her for at least a week.

Sylvie and Brooklyn start chatting about the abhorrent reading list for next semester while I sip my beer and glance around. There's probably a good thirty to forty people here. Like Brooklynsaid, pretty impressive considering most underclassmen have gone home for the summer. I'm curious to see what Ozona is like between June and August. It's my first time staying. Brooklyn and I lived on campus our freshman and sophomore years, so this was our first year living off campus. Our lease goes until we graduate, so there's no reason to move home when school's not in session. Besides, Brooklyn's parents have taken advantage of their empty nest and spend most of their time traveling abroad. She doesn't really have a reason to go home. And while my parents are great, I don't really need to spend any more summers under their well-meaning but suffocating thumbs.

There's a group of boys throwing things in one corner of the bonfire. Grass, hay, cans, alcohol. They holler when the flames rise and spit at them. One of them almost trips, narrowly missing a faceplant into the flames. His friends scream with laughter.

There's a couple making out in the bed of a truck not too far from us. And there are more couples staked out at various logs, lawn chairs, and wherever they can finagle a seat. But it's one couple in particular that catches my eye. One couple that is definitely not making out.

They're fighting. They're trying to hide it, but their bodies are stiff and their eyes are locked. She gestures. A violent flick of the wrist.

I can see the glare in her eyes from twenty feet away. I can tell he's sweating. His shoulders are hunched, he's shaking his head.

"It didn't mean anything," he says. I can't tell if I actually hear him, or if I just read his lips.

She snaps something back, shrill enough that I hear her voice, but not loud enough for me to make out words. Then he turns his head. Even without those stupid sunglasses, I recognize the face. Justin.

Damn. Jaclyn didn't take long to call him on his bullshit. And here? In public? That's . . . brave? Reckless? A little embarrassing? I don't know.

I lean forward, enthralled. I haven't seen many of my couples in person. My sad, unsuccessful couples who I break up. It's interesting. All I ever get is the assumption. I *assume* it's some big fight. Some huge confrontation. Maybe she barges into his apartment, screenshots in hand. Or maybe she calls him immediately.

But this is much more fun. Seeing it in person.

I feel almost a little bad. This shouldn't be entertaining. But honestly, Justin is getting chewed the fuck out right now, and it's a little satisfying. Jerk. I wish I was closer.

I feel Brooklyn leaning toward me.

"Is that . . ." she murmurs.

I nod. "Yep."

"Huh," she says. "Have you ever actually seen it go down like this?"

I shake my head.

Sylvie's attention has shifted to us. She follows our gaze. "You guys still doing that?" she asks. "Sarah?" She chuckles.

Sarah. The Instagram profile full of Brooklyn's photos and manned by me. Sarah. The fake girl countless guys have fallen for, to the demise of their "committed" relationships.

Brooklyn shrugs. "It's mostly Vally. I don't really participate much anymore."

"Except for your pictures," Sylvie points out.

She shrugs again.

"Is that . . . healthy?"

I shoot her a deadpan look. I can feel the judgment in her tone. "What, do you feel bad for those guys?"

"No." She shakes her head. "I guess they do deserve it." She pauses. "I would just feel bad *doing* it."

"Then I guess you're a better person than I am," I tell her. Brooklyn chuckles.

I glance back at the couple. Suddenly Jaclyn turns and storms off into the darkness. I expect Justin to go after her, but he just watches her go and slowly turns back to the flames in front of him. I suppose I shouldn't be surprised. What's he going to do? He's guilty of the crime. No amount of arguing will fix that.

I sip my drink again, glancing away from him. Show's over, I guess. Brooklyn and Sylvie have gone back to chatting about classes for next year. My phone buzzes in my pocket. It's an Instagram message. For Sarah.

The screen blinks up at me, almost bright enough to garner attention.

Hey. I heard you're the girl to talk to if you think your boyfriend is cheating.

I glance over at Brooklyn, and she rolls her eyes. She knows. I type back.

```
Sarah: Yeah. That's me.
```

Chapter 3

The front door to our apartment swings closed with a squeak. Brooklyn dumps her purse on our small, bright-pink entryway table, its contents jingling. She thrifted the table this summer and painted it, hoping it would bring some color to our old, drab, and honestly pretty basic apartment. It's the kind of apartment most college students have. But leave it to Brooklyn to bring in pink furniture and declare the problem solved.

"That was fun," Brooklyn states, heading to her bedroom to no doubt change into some form of loungewear.

I make some noncommittal noise in response. It was. Brooklyn mostly chatted with Sylvie the whole time while I people watched. Nothing was quite as interesting as watching Justin and Jaclyn's relationship blow up across the bonfire, but it was fine. Saw a couple boys drunkenly hurt themselves, saw lots of awkward flirting, and there was way too much making out to even count.

I follow Brooklyn's lead and head to my own room to change into pajamas. It's late, nearing one in the morning, but Brooklyn is still chatting with me, telling me about her day from across the hallway.

"My parents called this morning. They made it to Myanmar. Apparently, they'll be out of reception for a few days though. They're doing some rural hiking thing? Who knows with them?" She laughs. Her parents have taken advantage of their new empty nest syndrome and started traveling. Like, a lot. Everywhere. Their newest adventure was a trip through Asia. They started in Japan a few months ago and have apparently hit Myanmar.

"Sounds fun," I respond. "They better be bringing you a ton of cool souvenirs."

"I know they got me a bunch of cat stuff from Japan."

I laugh. If our landlord would allow it, Brooklyn would immediately add a cat to our family. Probably two. She volunteers at the local pet shelter in town on occasion, specifically in the cat rooms. She's sent me way too many pictures of cute kittens. Don't get me wrong: cats are great. I just don't need a picture every time Brooklyn comes into contact with one. It's endearing, though.

It's fun her parents are traveling. Mine are mainly homebodies. I grew up a few hours away from here in the tiny town of Belbridge. I visit occasionally, but haven't been back in a few months, now that I realize it. I should probably plan a summer trip.

I head to the kitchen for a glass of water, and Brooklyn's already there snacking on Goldfish. I fill up my glass, rubbing my lower back absentmindedly. It hurts from standing around the bonfire for hours. You'd think standing would have absolutely no effect—I mean, I'm literally doing nothing. But it often seems to bring on the worst pain.

Brooklyn's eyebrows knit together. "You need ibuprofen?" she asks. She knows I try to avoid the prescription meds I have on my bedside table if at all possible. I may be suffering from an actual medical condition, but it doesn't mean I want to actually admit it.

I shake my head and shoot her a grateful smile. "No, thanks." I'm also trying to avoid kidney failure if at all possible. I can't just take pain pills like they're M&Ms. Sometimes the pain is better than hypochondriac-induced anxiety.

"I saw Matt the other day," I say softly. I wasn't going to bring it up, but the way it's been eating at me for the past forty-eight hours makes me think it's probably something I need to air out. And Brooklyn is great at calming me down and putting things into perspective.

She stiffens and shoots me a sidelong glance. "Did you guys talk?"

I shake my head. "No. It was at the grocery store, and I just immediately left. I don't think I could handle talking to him."

She nods, biting the inside of her lip. "Not that you need to subject yourself to anything you don't want, but he's gotta know he was in the wrong. You're not the one who needs to feel ashamed or worried if you guys run into each other." She crosses her arms and leans back against the counter.

I nod slowly. She's right. Even if he denied it and gaslit me into oblivion, making me think that somehow his emotional cheating was my fault. Or that nothing happened in the first place. But hundreds of messages with some random girl on Instagram, including nudes, is not nothing. And to blame it on your girlfriend of two years is probably the shittiest way you could react to her finding out.

No. Matt is an asshole through and through, and somehow I doubt that he'll ever fess up to what he truly did. How he made me feel like shit for months. How I still feel like shit sometimes, years later.

And how I now make other men feel like shit for doing the same thing to their poor, unsuspecting girlfriends.

"He's the one who's going to keep tearing his life apart by acting like a child," Brooklyn tells me. "If he hasn't realized how awful he was to you yet, he's never going to have a fulfilling relationship with anyone." She squeezes my arm in comfort.

I grin halfheartedly. She's right. Like she always is.

Chapter 4

There's a permanent pink stain on the rug beneath my feet. As if some unfortunate employee was stabbed to death one day after a customer was given a smoothie that was not quite perfect. The real story is far less interesting.

Good thing customers can't see it as it's behind the counter, and all they get to see is my smiling face and a board behind me plastered with smoothie orders. I spilled a "Tropical Vacation" my first week working here, hence the stain that has yet to come out. But honestly, who buys a white rug for a smoothie shop? For any kind of food service establishment? If you ask me, that stupid rug was just an accident waiting to happen.

The bell above the door jingles, and I look up from my phone where I'd been mindlessly scrolling through social media.

A grin stretches across my face. Probably the first genuine one of the day. "Hey," I call as Brooklyn strides through the door. She makes her way past the empty neon-colored plastic tables and chairs and up to the counter. This is probably her favorite place in town. It's partially how I got the job. She spends so much money here that the manager loves her—who wouldn't? So, when I started job hunting, she pulled some strings and got me in. Not that it's the best job in the world, but it'll do for now.

She leans her elbows on the tall counter in front of me. "How's it going?" she asks, as if she hadn't seen me just a mere three hours ago at our apartment.

I shrug. "Fine. It's a slow day. Which is both great and mind-numbingly boring."

She laughs.

"Jungle Juice?" I ask. She nods. It's the one green smoothie drink we carry. And aside from the horrible name, it's actually not too bad. I used to scrunch up my nose whenever she'd appear with one in her hand. No matter how good it is, a green pile of gunk never looks that appetizing. It took her weeks to convince me to try it. And it's not awful. I mean, the berry mixes are definitely better, but Jungle Juice doesn't make me want to gag, so points there.

"So, are you helping out that new girl?" Brooklyn asks. She's referring to the one who messaged me last night at the bonfire.

I shrug. "Probably."

Brooklyn bites her lip in thought. "I've been thinking about what Sylvie said."

"What did she say? Sylvie says a lot of things."

She chuckles. "About this. The catching guys cheating thing."

I start grabbing ingredients for her drink. "What about it?"

She sighs. "I don't know."

I whip my head toward her from where I'm beginning to pour powders and veggies into the blender. "Do you agree with her? Are you starting to feel bad for them?"

She rolls her eyes. "I don't know. No. I mean, the guys are douchebags. You always make sure of that." She laughs. "I just . . . I wonder if it's good for us. For you. You're the one talking to them all day."

I press the blender button, and we halt our conversation as her smoothie materializes. She meets my gaze over the whirring of the blades, her thoughts practically colliding with mine. The blender ends, and I pour her smoothie into a cup.

"We can take your pictures down, if that's what you're worried about," I tell her, handing her the smoothie.

She shakes her head. "No, I don't care about that."

"Seriously, though. If you're ever uncomfortable about that, we stop. I can find other pictures. Other people. It doesn't have to be you."

She sips her drink. "I'm not worried about that. But doesn't it just . . ." She looks at me. "Doesn't it make you, I don't know, sad?"

My brows crinkle. "Sad?" I echo.

Her expression turns helpless. "Yeah. Like, dealing with other people's shit. Their unhealthy relationships that are falling apart. Doesn't that . . . bug you?"

"Honestly, no. I'm happy. I'm helping them," I tell her. The things I've told myself countless times. "Because if no one helps them, they'll end up staying in a relationship that's not real, with some asshole who's been cheating on them for *years*." The last word hitches in my throat, and I have to shove it out, breaking it to pieces along the way.

Brooklyn's eyes soften, and she lowers her gaze. "Yeah. I get that," she says quietly.

All of a sudden, I feel weird. Like I've just snapped at my best friend. "But if you don't want your pictures involved, we can take them down," I say again, my voice level. Even my smile is back.

She grins. "No. Seriously, it's fine." She hands me her credit card and her punch card for the smoothie. "Does stir fry sound okay for tonight?" she asks. "I'm heading to the store after this."

"Yeah, that sounds great," I tell her.

"Cool. See you later." She shoots me one of those Brooklyn smiles. The kind that crinkles around her eyes and lights up the room. The kind where you know she means it.

"See you," I call after her as she exits the shop.

My back hurts, so I sit on the small stool behind the counter and survey the empty room. It probably won't pick up for another hour or so. I pull out my phone to message Katie, the new girl wanting help with her boyfriend. From what I've deduced so far, it's the same old story. He's been distant, never wants to hang out. Promises nothing's wrong, but won't talk. She hasn't caught him cheating, so who knows, this might end well for her. Sometimes—rarely—the guys ignore my advances, and I get to send happy screenshots back to these girls. But that doesn't happen often. Happy girlfriends don't reach out to Instagram models asking them to catfish their boyfriends.

But when I open the app, a new message pops up. From some guy named Blaine. Blaine? I squint and open the message.

```
Blaine: You fucking piece of shit.
```

Well, get right to the point, why don't you? I narrow my eyes. Who is this guy? I click on the profile. Oh. Blaine. From about a month ago. I broke up him and his girlfriend after he sent me some dick pics and asked if I wanted to perform oral on him. Classy.

```
Blaine: You're a bitch, you know that?
```

I roll my eyes. Not that I disagree, but come on.

```
Sarah: All I did was show her who you really are.
```

I honestly don't even remember the girl's name.

```
Blaine: You don't know anything
about me.
    Sarah: Except for how small your
dick is.
```

This must make him mad. The "typing" sign appears and disappears several times.

```
Blaine: Watch your back. I'm
gonna fuck you up.
```

Not very nice, but okay. I roll my eyes and put my phone away. I've definitely argued with these guys in the past. Heated arguments. Usually just me mocking them while they rage. But I'm not in the mood for this right now. Blaine will get over it. It's his own damn fault. He just wishes he could blame it on me. As if he wouldn't have done the same thing to another girl if I hadn't been around.

I glance at the empty shop, at the door, at the street outside. My phone buzzes. Probably another message from Blaine.

I wonder if Brooklyn was right. Maybe things are getting out of hand.

Chapter 5

I fumble for my keys in my oversized purse as I make my way toward the apartment complex. It's surprisingly hot for June in Idaho. I'm sweating under my long-sleeved uniform shirt. The ones we all have to wear at the smoothie shop. I hate it. It's bright pink with fruit on it. I look like a seven-year-old.

I stop in front of the door, now fully digging through my purse. I sigh in exasperation. I'm just about to dump the contents of my bag onto the street, when I feel someone beside me.

"I got it," a voice says.

I look up, and my breath catches in my throat. I freeze, still elbow-deep in my bottomless pit of a bag.

Julian Sun. Writing 101. He sat in front of me freshman year, and I spent all semester staring at his back, at his hair, how he held his pencil in his hand. He smiles at me, his impossibly dark eyes glittering, swiping his key card. The door buzzes, and he opens it, gesturing for me to go in.

I smile back. "Thanks." Suddenly I'm all too aware of how sweaty I am, how awful this shirt looks. I stop in the entryway, pretending to check my mail in the boxes on the wall as he passes me, even though I know it's empty. He shoots me a shy grin before half walking, half jogging up the stairs. I watch his lean form and black head of hair disappear around the landing. I close my mail box and bite my lip, following him up the same stairs, slow enough that I know I won't run into him and he'll be gone by the time I reach my apartment.

I knew he lived here. I think he moved in at the beginning of last year like Brooklyn and I did. Most people in the complex are Idaho University students. I've seen him a handful of times. Passing each other in the lobby or grabbing our mail at the same time. We never really say anything. Just smile and move on. Like today.

I trudge up the stairs, my traitorous bag in hand. I still have to fish through it to find my apartment keys. When I finally make it through the front door, I drop my bag on the couch and start shedding clothing on my way to my room. The owners of the shop are cheap and don't believe in full air conditioning, meaning I'm a hot, sweaty mess every day after work. And my back hurts. Great.

Our apartment is small. Two bedrooms and a bathroom. Our living room and kitchen are combined, with a couch pushed up against the wall under the windows and a TV balanced on a small coffee table across from it. We don't have room for a dining table. We just eat on the couch. Or the floor. Or, when school is in session, on our way out.

I toss my clothes in the laundry pile in the corner of my room and search my drawers for some shorts and a T-shirt.

"Brooklyn? You here?" I call. She doesn't work today, so unless she's still out shopping, I assume she's probably in her room. I'm surprised I didn't find her vegged out in front of the TV.

Our rooms are right across from one another, but when I peek out, I notice that her door isn't shut. I step across the hallway, peering inside. "Brooklyn?"

Huh. I guess she really isn't here.

I make my way to the kitchen. It's about 5:15, and I'm starving. I might as well start on the stir fry thing she suggested earlier today. I search the fridge for ingredients but don't really find anything other than a dried-up, old broccoli from last week. She must not have gotten to the store yet. I grab a bag of chips from the cabinet and hop on the sofa.

I flip on the TV, pulling up a Netflix series I've been binging. Something about vampires. I pull out my phone, scrolling through Instagram and a few other social media apps. Blaine has continued to send me threatening messages, although they've let up the past couple hours. I'm just ignoring them now. It's not like I can accomplish anything by talking to him.

I think the girl from last night chickened out. She hasn't answered my last message, and I sent it early this morning. That happens. Sometimes girls are just pissed at their boyfriends and want to do something drastic. That might have been her. Who knows?

I watch an episode and a half of my vampire show. A couple people die, and at least one couple ends up having sex. Pretty typical of the genre. I've finished about half the bag of these chips, so I roll it up and put them away.

I pull out my phone, sending Brooklyn a text.

```
Vally: Hey, where are you?
```

My show is still playing, so I lie back down on the couch, my chin propped up on my palms. Ten minutes go by without a response from Brooklyn. I stare down at my phone and frown. She's usually pretty quick to reply. She's glued to her phone, like any good Gen Z kid. What is she doing?

Does she have a date I forgot about? Was she hanging out with Sylvie tonight? I swear she mentioned dinner earlier . . .

Maybe she forgot she had plans.

I give it another half hour before assuming dinner is off and heading to the kitchen to make something other than a bag of chips. We don't have a lot, but I find a packet of instant noodles in the pantry and boil some water. I go back to the couch, tucking my feet underneath me.

The vampire show is still going strong. The drama is intensifying. I don't know what it is about vampires, but God, their lives are melodramatic. Somebody fucked somebody else's girlfriend, and now they're on a killing rampage. Not to mention that someone else's brother just got turned into . . . another type of vampire? I'm not sure. It's confusing. Also, they're all, like, immortal. You'd think they'd have figured this shit out by now and be the most boring people ever.

Also, what's with all the eligible, hot, immortal vampires running around? Are you trying to tell me that after five hundred years of life, these people have yet to find someone to settle down with? That bodes . . . *terribly* for me.

Although I guess a show about boring, nonviolent, happily married vampires wouldn't be all that interesting.

An hour later, I still haven't heard from Brooklyn. I scrunch up my face. She must have a date. That's the only reason she wouldn't be checking her phone. Even with Sylvie, she'd still return my texts. Yeah, she must have a date. It's not unusual for some guy to ask her out. She's never really had a long-term relationship throughout college, but lots of guys want to date her. She's more in the "fun" stage than anything else. We've had a few double dates, typically set up by whoever she happens to be dating at the time. His friend and I tag along, and it's fine. I've had a hard time dating the past few years. Ever since—well, whatever.

So that must be it. A date. That she forgot to tell me about. Which, again, is unusual, but it's not like I'm her mother. She can do whatever she wants.

After another hour, the vampire show just gets irritating, and I turn it off. I glance at the clock. 8:30. If it's a date, it must be going well.

I stare down at my phone. Maybe she just didn't see my first text come through.

```
Vally: Hey! Did you have
something tonight that I forgot
about?
```

I try to not stare at my phone while I wait for her reply. I get up and do the dishes that have been sitting in the sink for way too long. A week maybe? I'm not sure. Neither Brooklyn nor I are the cleanliest of people. I dry the dishes and put them away. Then I organize the kitchen. There are dirty rags that need to be washed, so I pull new ones out of the drawer.

When I wander back to my phone lying on the couch, the screen is blank. Still no text from Brooklyn.

And that's when it sets in. Dread. I snatch up my phone.

```
Vally: Brooklyn. You're okay,
right?
```

I wait ten minutes before sending the next one.

```
Vally: Your phone better be dead
or something.
```

I pace the living area, shooting glances at my phone that won't buzz. It's probably nothing. Her phone died. She's out with friends. She's on a date. Or something else just as equally plausible. Normal. Fine. Safe.

Eventually, I head to bed. But I just lie there, staring at the ceiling, hoping to hear the door open and Brooklyn's feet padding across the hardwood.

When my phone buzzes, I practically launch myself out of bed and grab it off the nightstand. But it isn't Brooklyn.

```
Blaine: You'll see. You'll regret
this.
```

Chapter 6

I spend the night tossing and turning in bed, and by 4 a.m., I'm no longer able to sleep. By 4:30, I'm stress-cleaning the entire apartment. It has never looked so nice. Things are put away, the floor is swept and mopped, and I've dusted and wiped down every visible surface. Even some that aren't that visible. I even deep clean the bathroom—something Brooklyn and I usually flip a coin over.

6 a.m. rolls around, and I shoot Brooklyn another text. When she doesn't respond by 7, I text Sylvie.

```
Vally: Hi. Were you out with
Brooklyn last night?
```

She doesn't respond for forty-five minutes, which drives me insane, but when she does, it's unfortunately not very helpful.

```
Sylvie: No. Why?
Vally: She's not with you now?
Sylvie: No. Is something wrong?
```

I bite my lip. No. No, no, no. Nothing is wrong. Nothing is wrong. But Sylvie is the person she was most likely to be with. At least, she's the only friend of Brooklyn's whose number I have. And I don't have her parents' numbers either. They're out of the country for the summer anyway—currently in Thailand? Vietnam? I can't remember.

Maybe she was on a date. She has to have been on a date. A date that went really well. And she'll be showing up here in last night's clothes any minute now.

```
Vally: Do you happen to know if
she had a date last night?
```

It's stupid of me to involve her. She's just going to ask questions now. What am I doing, letting this freak me the fuck out like this? Now that I think about it, it has to have been just a date that went really well. It's not like she hasn't spent the night at a guy's place before.

```
Sylvie: Not that I know of.
You're her roommate. Wouldn't you
know?
```

Yeah, you'd think. Damn am I going to chew her out when she gets back. Nicely. But for real. I spent all night worrying about her. The least she could do was text me.

Vally: Just let me know if you hear from her.

I flop onto the couch, rubbing my lower back. The ache has intensified since yesterday. This happens, though. It comes and goes.

I was diagnosed with scoliosis as a teenager. A few surgeries and lots of pain medication later . . . I'm still in pain. All the time, pretty much. I'm used to it by now, though. It usually just fades into the background. When it gets super bad, though, I get a little cranky. I grab my heating pad from the basket next to the couch, plugging it in and leaning back against it. It takes a few minutes for the warmth to kick in, and I always doubt if it even does anything, but at least it's distracting.

Although not as distracting as I'd like it to be. As the minutes tick by, turning into hours, I bite my lip raw while watching the door. Where the fuck is she? I don't have work today, so I put on my vampire show again, but it doesn't do much to quell the anxiety.

Noon rolls around, and I feel like I'm talking myself off a cliff every second. I decide to text Brooklyn again.

Vally: Okay, I'm actually really worried now. Please respond?

As expected, I don't receive a reply. A knot forms in my stomach. I'm hungry, but there's no way in hell I can eat now. What happened? If her phone died last night, surely she's had time to charge it by now. Why won't she answer? If she spent the night at a guy's house, she'd be awake by now, right? She's been known to sleep to noon a handful of times, but still.

Suddenly I get up, grabbing my apartment keys and phone and heading out the door. I take the stairs two at a time and burst out into the midday sun. I jog around the side of the building to where the parking lot is. My car is where I left it last night. An old blue SUV. I scan the lot. Brooklyn's car is a small silver sedan. Usually she parks in the corner, shaded under the trees. I walk across the asphalt, peering over and around cars as I go. Halfway there, I stop in my tracks.

There it is. Brooklyn's car. Parked there like it always is.

And I stand there. Doing nothing. Because why would Brooklyn's car be here if she wasn't? Slowly, I move toward it. I don't know what I'm expecting to find. Brooklyn sitting there? Like normal? But I reach it and peer through the windows.

At first, I see nothing. Just some old coffee cups and a sweater. But then I glance at the backseat, and my breath catches in my throat.

Grocery bags. Full grocery bags. I exhale a shaky breath. She'd said she was going to the store. We were going to make dinner. I can see the ingredients through the white plastic. Veggies, chicken, coffee creamer because we were running low.

I feel like I'm going to vomit. Why would Brooklyn leave groceries in the car? Where would she go? She was obviously coming home, and then . . . what?

I pull my phone from my back pocket. My fingers are shaking so hard I almost drop it. I've never done this before, but I dial 911. A calm and cheery woman answers the line.

"I, um—" I choke out, still staring at Brooklyn's car. "I think I need to report a missing person."

Chapter 7

I sit on the couch, my knees pulled up to my chest, staring at the floor. My phone is lying face up beside me, and I'm praying that at any moment I'll receive a text from Brooklyn. That there's some normal reason for her being gone, for staying out all night, for abandoning her car full of groceries. For being so wholly unlike her . . .

But it stays silent. The police are coming by at some point. At least that's what they said. It's been two hours.

A loud knock on the door shakes me from my thoughts, and I scramble off the couch. Two policemen wait in the hallway, and I hurriedly let them in.

They stand at the threshold while one says, "Hello, ma'am, we were told you have a person to report missing?"

"Yes, my roommate," I say.

He nods, and they both enter the apartment. There's really nowhere to sit—with not owning a kitchen table and all—so we all kind of stand around awkwardly.

The second police officer must notice my nerves because he calmly offers, "You can take a seat if you'd like," gesturing to the couch.

I do, curling my legs underneath me. The officer has a pen and notebook out. "What's your roommate's name?" he asks.

"Brooklyn Fraser. She didn't come home last night. I thought maybe she was just out with friends, but she won't respond to my text messages, and it's just not like her. Her car is also in the parking lot, and there are still groceries inside. Like, new groceries. Perishables. She wouldn't leave those there. Something must have happened," I blurt out.

The officer is jotting things down on his notepad. He nods. "Does she have a boyfriend?"

I shake my head.

"Maybe a boyfriend you don't know about?"

"Unlikely."

"You're both students, correct?"

I nod.

He purses his lips. "College students stay out late all the time. Are you sure she wasn't just at a party last night?"

I frown. "I mean, it's possible, but she'd tell me. She's not responding, that's what's weird."

"It hasn't even been a full day," the officer says.

My frown deepens. What the hell? "She's not an airheaded college kid," I snap. "She's responsible. I'm telling you, something happened."

Both officers are nodding now, obviously detecting my change in attitude. "I understand," the first one says. "Do you have any photos of her?"

I reach for my phone, pulling open the photos app. "Tons," I say.

The second officer leans over, handing me a business card. "Email them to this address, and we'll add them to the case file."

Case file. For some reason, all that conjures up are dusty cabinets and photos of missing girls that no one will ever find. I swallow. "Okay."

They ask me a few more questions, jotting down my answers and nodding along as if they care. I voluntarily tell them about the account we run together—earning me a hard look from one of the officers. They ask for the account access, but don't seem all that impressed. Eventually, one says, "Thank you, Ms. Evans. Please reach out if you think of anything else to add." They move toward the door.

I stand. "You'll look for her, right?"

One turns and nods at me. "We'll do our best."

I follow them, almost in desperation. There has to be more. More that they can do. More that I can do. But they're just walking away. With their little notes jotted down on that stupid pad of paper and my photos waiting in an email inbox that probably won't be checked for hours. Days maybe. While Brooklyn is . . .

Who knows? And that's the goddamn point.

I follow them to the door and watch them retreat down the hallway, disappearing around the corner, their footsteps echoing down the stairwell.

Panic is setting in. Because if the police won't do anything, who will?

Just then, I feel something. Pressure, energy, someone's eyes on me. My gaze slides to the right and collides with someone else's. Julian Sun. He's standing by the door to an apartment that must be his, keys in hand. I'd never realized how close we lived. Just a few doors down from one another.

There's a question in his eyes. No doubt he saw the police officers leaving.

His hand drops to his side. "Is everything okay?" he asks. It might only be the fourth or fifth thing he's ever said to me. But it isn't nosey. Or at least it doesn't sound like it. He seems legitimately concerned.

Suddenly I realize how open I am. What my face must look like. How I watched the officers go, on the verge of a breakdown. Normally, I've got my guard up. I'm cold, unapproachable, an expression not worth reading.

I swallow. "Yeah. Um. Kind of." I'm pulling layers back up, one at a time. But it feels weird to lie. What can I say? The police were just stopping by?

Julian takes a hesitant step toward me, then gives in and just walks over. "What's going on?" he asks softly. He's still a respectable five feet away, but he feels so close. This is closest we've ever stood. Other than passing in the lobby, him holding the door for me yesterday.

I just stare at him for a heartbeat. "My . . . roommate," I breathe. "She—she didn't come home last night. Or today. She's probably fine, I just . . ."

His eyebrows raise. "You can't get ahold of her?"

I shake my head. We stand in silence for a moment, and I stare down at my shoes. Then his shoes. Nice shoes. Nike sneakers. Blue.

"Is it just you two?" he asks.

I look up. "Yeah." There's an uncomfortable pause before I purse my lips and shoot him a tight smile. "I should—" I start, stepping back into my apartment.

"Wait," Julian says, taking a small step forward.

I stop, turning to him.

"Are you sure you're okay being alone?"

I almost laugh at the question. Me being alone is what I'm good at. Me being alone is what I assumed college would be like until Brooklyn came around. But honestly, the idea of me being along right now is sending my stomach into knots.

"Do you want to get something to eat?" he asks when I don't reply. He must notice my questioning stare, as he quickly adds, "I, just—have you eaten much today?"

I haven't. I haven't eaten anything. Not even coffee. I've been upset. Too worried, too stressed. And even now, the thought of food makes me feel sick, but the thought of walking back into my apartment alone makes me feel sicker.

I shake my head. "I mean, no, I haven't eaten today. I should eat." I nod. "I should."

Julian smiles. It's small, but his eyes sparkle just a little. "Okay. Good. We should go eat something."

Chapter 8

Julian suggests the Denny's across the street, so about five minutes later, we find ourselves sitting in the corner booth, gazing down at their large, intimidating menu. Even with the distraction of another person, though, I can barely stomach eating. I grimace down at the options.

I feel Julian's stare and glance up to meet his gaze.

"You should eat," he repeats, as if reading my mind. "Even if it's only a little."

I nod. He's right. I am hungry. I can feel it clawing at my insides. But along with the gnaw of hunger is nausea. Both at the fact that Brooklyn is missing, and that I'm sitting here. With Julian Sun. The one guy in my entire college experience that I have found even vaguely attractive. And I don't even know why. It's not like he's that good looking or anything. He's probably about five-ten or so and lanky, most likely doesn't work out. His hair is a little too long, and he has this dumb, lopsided smile. I probably only find him attractive because he's smart.

Or at least I think he's smart. He sounded smart when he'd raise his hand in class, bring up discussion points, ask questions. Honestly, he gives off the vibe of a total nerd. Quiet, reserved, not a lot of friends.

Like me.

"What are you getting?" I ask.

He shrugs. "Maybe this burger." He points.

I nod in agreement. I sigh. "I don't know. Nothing looks good. I mean, they look good, just . . ."

Julian's smile falters. "Yeah," he says. "Here, just order a burger, try to eat what you can, and take the rest home."

I agree, and when the server comes to take our order, we get burgers and iced tea. And suddenly we're sitting in silence, staring at the table. I bite the inside of my lip, glancing up at him every few seconds.

"I think we were in Writing 101 together. Freshman year," I finally say.

"I know."

He knows? That means he remembered me. And I'm not all that memorable. What does he remember? Was I cute as a freshman? Probably not.

He was the first guy I had a crush on after Matt. After he stomped my heart and dignity into the ground halfway through freshman year. And then all my attention shifted to Julian—building him up in my head as this adorable, perfect man who could never break anyone's heart, too afraid to actually approach him and risk that fantasy shattering to pieces.

"Yeah, you were quiet. You sat in the back." He's smiling, but then he shakes his head. "Sorry. That's not a bad thing. It sounded like a bad thing. I didn't mean it like that."

"No, it's fine. I remember the professor always liked you. He'd call on you a lot."

Julian shrugs. "I'm good at BSing my way through answers." He chuckles.

"It's a good skill to have."

He grins. "So, what's your major?"

"Accounting." Numbers, analytics, logical thinking. Less people skills and more . . . things I understand, I guess. "What about you?"

"Well, I started in English. Wanted to be a journalist or a writer or something. But now I'm a business major." He shrugs. "We'll see what happens."

"How long have you lived in the apartment building?" I ask.

"We moved in at the beginning of last year."

"Same," I reply. "I'm surprised we didn't run into each other while moving in. Also, I had no idea we lived so close. I mean, I've seen you around but—didn't realize you're like two doors down." It dawns on me that I'm close to rambling. Also, we don't even know each other. Why would I be wondering about how close he lives to me? Shut up, Vally. Shut up.

"Yeah, we tend to pass each other in the lobby quite a lot," he says with a smile. "I might have seen you coming out of your apartment once? I don't know."

Again. He remembered. "So, you have a roommate?"

He nods. "Yeah. Carter. He's fine. We were kind of just acquaintances before we moved in together. We both needed a roommate." He pokes at the ice in his water with a straw. "It's weird, right?" he asks, looking up. "How you end up living with complete strangers."

I nod along. "College is weird."

Our food comes not long after, and I nibble at my burger, mainly just eating a few fries. I notice Julian does something similar. "You not hungry either?" I ask.

He looks almost embarrassed that I've noticed. "Oh. Um, yeah."

I purse my lips together. I try to eat a few more fries, watching Julian out of the corner of my eye. Is he . . . nervous? It suddenly dawns on me. The way he's sitting—stiff and straight. How he keeps fidgeting with his iced tea, twirling the ice cubes around with his straw. Picking at his food, glancing at me when he thinks I'm not looking.

Oh my God. He's nervous. Why is he nervous? What could he possibly have to be nervous about? Me? I am literally the most unintimidating person alive.

Well, okay, that's not true. I can be damn intimidating when I want to be. But not in the way that girls are supposed to be intimidating to guys. Not in the way Brooklyn walks down the hallway and men melt. In the way that makes them just stare from afar, speak too quickly, and do stupid things. I am most certainly not . . . that.

"Do you have summer plans?" I ask.

He bobs his head in a noncommittal way. "I'm not sure. I might go home to see family. I was thinking about making a fun road trip out of it. Stop at Yellowstone. Craters of Moon. Something like that."

"You should. Craters of Moon is actually pretty cool." I grin. "I went there with my parents as a kid. Who knows, though? Maybe I'm remembering it with rose-colored glasses. It might be boring and terrible."

He laughs. "Well, I'll just have to go and let you know."

I smile. "Yeah."

We end up picking away at our burgers and fries, making slow but noticeable progress, until well after the sun goes down. We watch the dinner rush come and go, all the while sipping iced teas and talking about school, family, friends, and video games. Apparently, Julian is also into *The Sims* and spends his free time creating families whose lives he can destroy. Who would've thought? Such an innocent face.

"I know that Denny's are typically open 24/7, but our server has been giving us the side eye for the past half hour," Julian leans over and murmurs to me.

I follow his gaze. "Yeah, I'd kind of noticed that too." It is late. It's dark outside. We've been here for hours. I sigh, the weight of today falling back on my chest, ready to suffocate me and all this food I just ate.

We leave our table, pay up front, and head out into the night. We cross the street and enter the complex in silence. I follow Julian up the stairs, the floorboards creaking beneath our feet as we walk. I almost have these creaks memorized by now. You step here, here, there, there, and I know the cacophony of sounds it'll make.

Julian walks me to my door. Which isn't exactly organic, since my apartment is past his.

I turn to look at him. "Thank you," I admit. "This was actually really helpful." It's all I can manage to say, but it's true. I think I needed to just talk. About anything. I think I might've gone crazy in my apartment alone. I might still go crazy. I *am* about to walk back in. The thought sends a dagger of dread through my stomach.

"Are you going to be okay?" Julian asks.

I shrug. No. "Yeah."

I know he doesn't believe me. "Okay."

There's a long stretch of silence.

"You could . . ." he trails off. "I hope they find her. They'll find her. Don't worry. Um—have a good night." He shoots me one last smile before heading down the hall. I watch him for the briefest of moments before hurrying into my apartment and shutting the door.

Chapter 9

I'm not sure what I expected. Maybe I watch too many true-crime documentaries and detective shows. And honestly, shame on me for believing anything about any of that was real. Because apparently the police don't give a shit about missing people. At least missing adults. Missing college students who are probably out partying. No. They have better things to do. Like give out speeding tickets to old ladies going five miles over the limit.

My shift at the smoothie shop was early today. I opened, but I get off at noon. And something about waking up to an empty apartment, putting on that stupid fruity T-shirt, and driving into work like nothing has happened is making me want to break my head open against a brick wall. Let my brains slide down the linoleum and mix with all the orange juice and fruit I've spilled on the floor. Because what the actual fuck?

It doesn't help that this was the last place I saw Brooklyn.

I end up calling the police station during my first break, but they are less than helpful. No. Worse than that. Discouraging. Heartbreakingly so. They haven't found her. They don't have any leads. And they don't sound like they're trying all that hard.

Fuck them.

When my shift ends, I drive home, furious. Because anger is better than drowning in worries and having a complete mental breakdown, right? Of course it is.

I throw my purse against the couch with a smack, my keys falling to the floor alarmingly loudly. "Goddammit, Brooklyn!" I yell. "Where are you?" I sink to a crouch, leaning against the coffee table, pulling my knees to my chest.

I will not cry. I will not cry. Get it together, Valerie. Get your shit together. Because if the police don't give a fuck, then somebody has to.

I wrack my brain for anything. *Anything*. Were there people who didn't like her? Seems impossible—she's a fucking Disney princess. Was there anything strange going on lately? Did she say anything weird? Did someone else say anything weird?

Suddenly breath hitches in my throat, and I turn my head. My phone is lying halfway out of my purse, on the couch. I don't know why I hadn't thought of it before, but it suddenly all makes sense. I lunge forward, scrambling across the floor, reaching for my phone.

Blaine.

I open Instagram, pulling up the messages he'd sent. A barrage on Sunday, ending with *You'll see. You'll regret this*. Those messages were sent to Sarah. Our perfect Instagram blonde. But Brooklyn is the face. Brooklyn is the girl he saw when sending those messages. The girl he now hates. I check the message receipts again, even though I know when they were sent. Sunday. The day Brooklyn went missing.

I sit back on my heels, staring at the screen.

Would he be crazy enough to do something like that? Is he that mad that he'd go out of his way to hurt her? Kidnap her? That's crazy, insane. But . . .

Brooklyn is gone. And this is all I have.

I stare at the screen some more. Because, what now? What do I do with this? I suppose I could bring this to the police. This is probable cause, right? A reason for them to question him? But honestly, would they even do anything about it? Based on their track record so far, I'm willing to bet their interest level would be a big fat zero.

I take a deep breath, exhaling through my nose.

```
Vally: What the fuck did you do?
```

I send the message, staring at the screen for way too long before realizing that he's not going to respond right away. He hasn't even seen the message. But it doesn't take too long. Ten minutes later, he replies.

```
  Blaine: What? Nothing. You're the
one messing up people's lives.
  Vally: Where is Brooklyn?
  Blaine: What are you talking
about?
```

I glare down at the screen. I should've known he'd pull this card. Of course he's not going to admit it. Why would he?

```
  Vally: Listen, you asshole.
You're not going to get away with
whatever the hell you're doing.
Where is she?
  Blaine: You're insane.
```

I resist the urge to chuck my phone at the wall.

```
  Vally: Tell me, and I won't tell
the police.
```

There's a long pause before he responds. Long enough that I think he might actually cave.

```
  Blaine: You're one crazy bitch,
you know that?
```

Crazy bitch. What Matt called me when I accused him of cheating. Only I wasn't crazy. I was right.

I grip the phone in my hand, wishing it was Blaine's neck and I could strangle him. But I'm not surprised. What, did I really think he would just admit it over text? Come clean? *Oh, sorry, here she is.*

But it has to be him. It has to be. He was angry. Raging. He sent Sarah nearly a dozen harassing messages. He threatened her. Threatened Brooklyn. And now she's gone. And it's my job to get her back.

I glare down at Blaine's messages before pulling up his Instagram profile. Blaine Hendersen. Based on his name, I'm able to find his Facebook profile which has a bit more information about him. He's twenty-one. He goes to Idaho University, majoring in Computer Science. His profile still lists him as in a relationship with his girlfriend, Katya. I wonder if that's true or if they just haven't made their breakup public yet. It looks like they were together awhile. At least a year.

He's from Boise, but moved here for college. But where does he live now? Not in the dorms, I'm assuming. He's an upperclassman. I search his name and end up finding his phone number, attached to his parents' names as well. Michael and Rachael Hendersen. But that's not all that useful. I search his number, hoping to find a residence somewhere, but nothing comes up. I'm able to find the address of his parents' homes in Boise, but not his here in Ozona. Which makes sense. It's temporary housing. He's a college student. His permanent residence is probably still his parents' house, just like mine is. Like Brooklyn's is.

I go back to Instagram. I check his story. It's him and some other guy playing a video game. *Call of*

Duty from the looks of it. I scroll through his feed. Not a ton of activity. He goes fishing a lot, it seems. There are quite a few pictures of him holding up dead fish with a stupid grin on his face. Congratulations, you beat an animal an eighth of your size. There is someone who keeps showing up in the photos, though. I'm willing to bet it's the same guy from the story. I scroll a ways down further and find a better photo. Blaine and a few other guys standing outside one of the dorms. Maybe it was move-out day. I tap the photo and grin when I see that his friend is tagged.

Sam Dodgen. His profile is much more colorful. Damn, he must post, like, almost every day. Lots of photos of his car. A little red something. I don't know. I don't know cars. But by the looks of it, this car is his baby. And his baby is . . .

Bingo. Sitting outside his house. The house I'm assuming he rents with Blaine. I tap on the image, zooming in to see the street number painted on the siding. I'm not sure of the street name, but the house and the yard look familiar. Ozona isn't that big, and there are only so many neighborhoods surrounding the university. I'm willing to bet I know what street this house is on.

And Blaine better be fucking ready.

```
Vally: This is your last chance.
```

He responds two minutes later.

```
Blaine: You're a psycho.
```

Typical. I screenshot the Instagram photo with the house number. He wants to see a psycho bitch? I'll show him one.

Chapter 10

I'm practically out the door, purse and car keys in hand, when I realize that stalking a man twice my size who's threatened me and potentially kidnapped my roommate might not be the best idea I've ever had.

At least, not alone.

I stand on the threshold, door halfway open, and my gaze slides down the hallway. I bite my lip. It's not like I'm going to confront Blaine. At least, I don't think so. I just need to watch him. Catch him in the act. Not unlike how I catch men in the act all the time. Only this is much more dangerous. Obviously. And what if I do catch him red-handed? What am I going to do? Run into the house alone?

No. I need someone to go with me. At least as a witness.

I glance at his door. I'm not even sure if he's home. Why would he be home? It's 1 p.m. on a Tuesday. He's probably working. And why would he even agree to come along? What would I say?

But he did take me to dinner last night. He sat with me for hours. He's the only person who knows that Brooklyn is missing. I suppose Sylvie might have an idea after my cryptic texts. But it's not like I'm going to ask her to come along—she'll only be more difficult than helpful.

He's the only conceivable person I *could* ask. It's him or no one.

I shut the door behind me, locking it. I walk slowly down the hall, stopping in front of Julian's door. I take a deep breath. He's probably not home. In which case, I'd honestly just go alone. Damn the consequences. It's partially my fault if it is Blaine who kidnapped her. I have to do this. The thought of Brooklyn spurs me on, and before I can stop myself, I raise my hand and knock.

Seconds tick by. I'm suddenly nervous. A few seconds more, and I assume he either didn't hear, or he isn't home. I'm just about to knock once more, for good measure, when the door swings open, and there stands Julian. He's wearing sweatpants and a T-shirt, and he has glasses on. And holy hell, he looks . . . cute. In glasses. Why does he look cuter in glasses? Also, I've never seen him wear them. He must wear contacts when he goes out. I'm not sure why, though, because this is a good look on him.

But, God, that doesn't matter right now.

His eyes widen in surprise when he sees me, and a second later, he smiles. "Vally," he says, almost like a question.

"Hey."

He opens the door wider. "How are you doing? Have they found Brooklyn?"

I shake my head. "No. Not yet. I'm okay."

His eyebrows furrow. "I'm sorry." His dark eyes are so compassionate, he practically looks like a wounded puppy. "Did you sleep last night?"

It's such a sweet question, that it momentarily catches me off guard. Sleep? He cares if I slept? I shrug in answer. "Not the best, no."

He nods.

"I, actually—I have something to ask you," I blurt out before I lose my nerve. Honestly, I was kind of expecting him to be out. I'd knock on the door, tell myself I tried, and then go off on my own. But here he is, and now I have to explain. There's no going back now.

He raises his eyebrows.

"This is going to sound crazy," I admit.

He tilts his head.

"I was wondering—well . . ." I sigh, biting the bullet. "I think I know what could have happened to Brooklyn. There's this guy I want to . . . watch. Do you want to come with me?"

Julian stares me down for a beat, his expression unreadable. But then his face softens. "Yeah," he finally says. "Yeah, okay."

"I know where he lives," I go on, realizing I sound like some creepy stalker. But I promised Blaine a psycho bitch, and here she is. If he did, indeed, kidnap Brooklyn, there's a whole lot more than stalking that he should be worried about from me.

"We can go now. If you're free?"

Julian nods. "Yeah." He's beginning to sound like a broken record. He still seems a little nervous. Kind of like last night. Although, I can't tell if they're leftover nerves, or something else entirely. Maybe he's afraid of me now. The stalker neighbor. This is admittedly a pretty creepy endeavor I'm propositioning him for.

This was insane. Why did I think of involving him? I'm just about to backtrack, come up with some excuse to go alone, when he whirls around, grabs his keys and wallet off a table nearby, and steps out into the hallway.

"Are you driving, or should I?"

"I will drive," I manage to utter. "Let's go."

Five minutes later, we're sitting in my blue 2000 Dodge Durango, crawling down Pearson Street on the other side of town, the Beach Boys playing at medium blast.

"The Beach Boys, huh?" Julian asks from the passenger seat.

I cringe at him. "Yeah. It got stuck in the CD player. It's the only thing that plays."

He nods with a smirk. "Didn't say it was bad."

"It gets bad right around the thirty-thousandth time you hear it," I inform him.

"Good to know."

We continue on in silence, "Surfin' USA" blasting through the speakers. I keep glancing down at my phone, screenshot in hand. The car is a sporty red thing, and the house looks like any normal suburban dwelling. Cream siding with a green door.

"Do you know where you're going?" Julian asks. He's peering at my phone in my lap, trying to not look obvious. I realize there's no use in keeping him in the dark. He's already here, so I hand him my phone.

"This is the house we're looking for. I have the number, there." I point. "But I don't know the street name."

He squints down at it. "This could be anywhere."

"Yeah, but I feel like it's in this neighborhood. See those trees in the background? I haven't seen those anywhere else."

He cocks his head, clucking his tongue. "I suppose."

"Just keep an eye out for a house that looks like that. And the car too."

We continue down the street, me scanning the left side while Julian scans the right. We come to a three-way stop, and I arbitrarily take a right. We can always circle back if we need to.

"So, who is this person we're looking for?" Julian asks.

I hesitate, but decide there's really no use in beating around the bush. "Blaine Hendersen. He's a student too."

There's a pause before Julian continues, "Why him?"

Now this is where my line is drawn. I'm not sure I'm ready to tell him about Sarah. About my strange little hobby that might have seemingly ruined my and Brooklyn's lives. "I have my reasons," I answer, and Julian takes the hint.

Suddenly I feel him tapping my arm, and I'm almost too startled by the fact that this is the first time he's touched me to realize that's he's pointing out the window. "That house," he says. "Is that it?" He holds up my phone for me to see the picture again.

I slam on the breaks, and Julian almost drops my phone. "Sorry," I say. I lean across the console and immediately I know this is the one. There's the little red car parked in the driveway. There's the white house with the green door. And there's the number painted on the building. 4708.

Adrenaline courses through me, and I punch the gas. Julian scrambles to hold on to something. I reach the end of the road and make a U-turn, driving back toward the house and parking on the other side of the street a few houses down. Close enough to see the house, but far enough away that hopefully my car doesn't look suspicious. I cut the engine, ending the Beach Boys' crooning. The silence envelops us as I lean forward over my steering wheel, still in disbelief that we've found it.

"So, what now?" Julian whispers.

I don't know. I don't know at all. I hadn't really thought this far. I've found Blaine's house. I know where he lives. But what do I do with that? It's not like I can go barging in. Not that it would accomplish anything unless Brooklyn happens to be sitting there in his living room.

"I want to watch the house," I eventually reply. "I need to make sure he lives here. And I need to watch for—something, anything."

Julian nods.

After a few minutes of intense staring, we both start relaxing back into our seats. Once again, I'm not sure what I expected, but watching a building is boring as hell. Eventually I kick my feet up over the steering wheel and dash and lean my seat back a tad. My scoliosis makes weird positions often the most comfortable. And I've lost any and all self-consciousness about it. If others were in pain all the time, they'd do the same.

"How'd you meet Brooklyn?" Julian asks at one point.

I bite my lip, unsure if talking about her will make me feel better or worse. "We met freshman year. She was my assigned roommate in the dorms."

"Wow, and you guys hit it off?"

I nod.

"That's rare. A lot of times those roommate situations can blow up. Or at least become somewhat contentious."

I laugh. "Is that what happened to you?"

He shakes his head. "No, we got along fine. Didn't really become friends though."

I stare out the window, my eyes locked on the street, the house, the car. "Yeah. She's the last person I ever would've thought to be my best friend," I admit. "She's so unlike me."

"How so?"

"She's just . . . good." It's all I can muster. All I can say. Brooklyn summed up in the simplest way possible.

I can feel Julian's gaze on me, but I refuse to turn and look at him. "This shouldn't have happened," I almost whisper. I can practically feel him boring holes through my skull. But just as I see him move in my peripheral, just as he's about to, what, I'm not sure—reach out and touch me?—a truck rolls down the street, pulling into the house's driveway, right alongside the red car.

"Oh my God!" I whisper yell, and Julian and I duck at the same time, almost crashing our heads together over the console.

I peer over the dash, watching as Blaine hops out of the truck, slamming the door closed and walking up to the house. He stands there for a moment, searching for a key, and then he disappears inside.

So, he does live here. This *is* his house.

Julian and I stay crouched over the console for a few heartbeats more. He's close enough that I can smell his shampoo. It smells like apples. His glasses are rimmed with blue. I hadn't noticed before now.

"I don't think he'll be coming back out," Julian says, slowly straightening in his seat.

I do the same.

"Was that him?"

I nod. "Yeah. Definitely."

"Okay. So, we accomplished one thing," he continues encouragingly. "We know for sure that this is where he lives."

I grin at him. He's trying to make me feel better. But surprisingly, seeing Blaine hasn't given me the vindication I was hoping for. Because now what? We just have to keep watching. We have to actually *catch* him doing something. But what?

My back is hurting from sitting in this car for too long. Although it tends to hurt no matter what I do, so I try to ignore it. We continue to watch the house. Again, nothing all that exciting happens. Blaine has arrived home. That's it.

After a while, Julian breaks the silence. "When you mentioned that Brooklyn was good," he says, "you sort of implied that you . . . weren't."

My gaze darts to his. The sun has lowered over the horizon by now, sending golden light into the cab of the car. It lights up his hair, his eyes, the console between us.

"Why do you say that?" he asks when I don't respond.

I continue staring him down, contemplating his question, until I realize that I have almost no idea what my expression is. It's probably somewhat intense. Intimidating. Angry, even. I shake my head. I sigh. "I don't know. She's just—she's kind and happy and cares about everything and everyone. I'm not like that." I bark out a laugh. "And if I'm right about what happened to her"—I look back at the house—"then it's my fault."

It's the first time I've said it out loud. The first time I've admitted what's been eating me alive since the moment I knew something was wrong. I'm the girl he's mad at. I'm the girl who ruined his relationship, who baited him into cheating, who fought with him over text. *I'm* the girl he wants. Not Brooklyn.

But, of course, how could he know that?

"Your fault?" Julian's voice is soft, like he couldn't possibly believe me.

I shake my head again. "It doesn't matter."

Julian's expression is one of sadness. Compassion, even. I can see it in his eyes. *It's not your fault*. And I know why he thinks that. Because what small, cute, harmless twenty-year-old girl could ever do anything bad? I may be slightly out of practice when it comes to boys, but I know why he's here. Why he had dinner with me last night. He likes me. Just like I've liked him. And the way he's looking at me now, the girl he gets to save while she searches for her lost best friend, is heartbreaking. Because he believes the best in me. I can see it in his face.

But I know it won't last. Or at least, it never could. He could never truly like me if he knew what I'd done. What I do every day. Because I'm not a good person. I'm not a *nice* person. I'm not the one who needs saving; Brooklyn is. And once he realizes that, this spell will be broken. He could never really care about me. Nobody could.

Chapter 11

Night falls, and despite Julian's subtle remarks about how late it's getting and how we should head home, I don't let us go. He signed up for this. Albeit without a ton of information, but nevertheless, he's here with me, and he's going to see this whole thing through. When 9:30 p.m. rolls around and most of the lights in the house have been off for at least half an hour, I turn to Julian to state my newly developed plan.

"I want to go inside."

He stares back blankly at me through the shadows. "What?"

"It's the only way to know for sure if Brooklyn's in there."

Both panic and confusion washes over Julian's features. "But—what even makes you so sure she's in there?"

"Like I said, I have my reasons," I snap back.

He groans but abruptly halts when I open my door and hop out. "What are you doing?" he hisses, scrambling after me, shutting the car door as quietly as he can and running across the pavement to catch up.

I've had enough time to formulate some sort of plan while we've been sitting in the dark. "I'm going to try the back door," I tell him.

"And just walk in . . . ?" Julian asks incredulously, temporarily grabbing my hand in an effort to slow me down.

"It's Idaho. Nobody locks their back doors. And if that doesn't work, we'll try a window."

Julian puffs out some noise of exasperation, but continues to keep up as I stride down the sidewalk toward Blaine's house. I cut across his lawn, ducking below a row of dark windows, and quickly make my way to the back of the house. I spot a sliding glass door, and just like the other windows of the house, it's dark.

"Vally. This is very illegal," Julian hisses from behind me, his voice a much higher pitch than I've ever heard from him before. It'd be funny if I was in a different headspace. But right now, I'm just angry and determined.

"So is kidnapping," I snap back.

"Which we don't know he's guilty of!"

I spin around, silencing him with a glare. "Which is why we're going to *find out*."

He sighs angrily, shaking his head in resignation.

I turn back to the door, grasp the handle, and gently pull. The door slides open with a soft hiss. Adrenaline hits my bloodstream so fast I almost stagger backward. Because Julian is right. This is crazy. Illegal.

But the thought of what Brooklyn could be going through—what women go through every fucking day and nobody gives a shit about—spurs me forward. I'd rather rot in a jail cell than potentially let a kidnapper get away with snatching my best friend.

I slide the door open just enough to squeeze inside. After a heartbeat, Julian follows.

The house is dark. Blaine and his roommate must be asleep. Or at least in their rooms. I glance around. It's the typical college living space. Old Craigslist furniture, dishes piled in the sink, clutter adorning the tables and counters. There's a kitchen to my left, a dining table to my right, and the living area is straight ahead.

I make my way forward slowly, letting my eyes adjust to the darkness. I use the dim light of my phone to scan the room. A jackpot would be finding Blaine's cellphone. Or even Sam's. But I'm sure those are in their rooms with them.

Just then, a railing catches my eye. To the left is a carpeted stairway leading down. I make a beeline to it. Julian's hushed, anxious footsteps pitter after me. In the soft glow of my phone, I see a room littered with boxes. Empty boxes. Must be leftover from moving.

Across the room is a door. I tiptoe over, pressing my ear against the wood, trying to discern whether this is a bedroom or not. There was a hallway upstairs, where I assumed both Blaine's and Sam's bedrooms would be, but I'm not certain.

Although, this door doesn't seem like a bedroom door. It's a cheaper wood, and based on how cold it is down here, I'm willing to bet this is just the basement and nothing more. I hold my breath, turn the knob, and push.

A rush of cool air greets me, along with a vast, empty space of darkness. I take a step forward, and the floor is concrete. Definitely not a bedroom. I grope along the walls until I find a light switch, and the room hums to life.

It's made up of concrete floors and uninsulated wood walls. There are some shelves in the corner with paint cans, brushes, and a myriad of other random supplies. But other than that, the room is empty.

Something like disappoint swarms in my gut. But what was I expecting? To find Brooklyn tied up in a corner like those stupid psychological thrillers on TV? That would certainly be easier. Then we could just sneak back out, call the police, turn Blaine in, and it'd be all over with.

I just want this to be fucking over with.

I angrily switch off the light, swirling and almost running into Julian's chest. "There's nothing here," I mutter under my breath, sidestepping him.

He nods. "Can we get out of here now?"

I don't answer. I just head back through the room and up the stairs. We tiptoe back to the living room, and I take once last glance around. For anything incriminating. Anything at all. Praying to a god I've ignored for most of my life that something will pop out at me and help me save Brooklyn's life.

But just as we're about to turn and go, a door creaks open, and Julian's hand brushes against my shoulder. We simultaneously spin as light pools on the hallway floor, spilling out, out, out toward the living room.

I back up, pulling Julian with me, until we're in the far corner. Maybe he's just getting up for a glass of water. He'll wander right by us and not even notice.

But that hope dies just as quickly as it was born when a voice calls out, "Hello?" It's tinged with fear but masked with assertiveness. And out into the light steps Blaine. He's wearing a ratty T-shirt and a pair of workout shorts, his eyes ping-ponging as he surveys the room.

Suddenly the overhead light flicks on, and Julian and I blink at the harsh glow. For half a second, I consider running—making a break for the nearest door. But it's useless. Besides, with both of us, Julian would probably be the one Blaine ends up catching.

"The fuck?" Blaine snaps, whirling toward us. "Who the hell are you?"

Julian begins stammering something nonsensical, but I cut him off. "You really don't know?" I level at him, letting my anger override any fear I'm currently feeling.

Blaine narrows his eyes, then shrugs. "What, are you some girl I banged once? You pissed I never called or something?"

I snort. "You wish. Does the name Brooklyn ring a bell?"

His confused expression deepens. "Did I bang *her*?"

"Fuck you!" I yell.

Just then, a soft noise comes from down the hallway, and Sam wanders into view. He glances at Blaine, then at us. "What's . . . going on?" he asks.

"Beats me," Blaine answers.

"How about the name Sarah?" I try, and I can't help the small twinge of satisfaction I feel when an irritated recognition washes over Blaine's features.

"What about Sarah?" he says slowly.

"Oh, so you know who I'm talking about now?"

"Yeah, the psycho bitch who ruined my relationship." There he goes again with that term of endearment. And the lack of accountability. A great combination, really. A real catch. "Wait," he mutters, the pieces slowly falling into place. "She texted me the other day. Mentioned something about a Brooklyn . . ." He trails off for a minute, then demands, "Who are you?"

"I *am* Sarah, you piece of shit. And Brooklyn's the one in the photos."

He tilts his head incredulously.

"She went missing a few days ago. Know anything about that?"

His expression darkens, and suddenly he just looks done with the conversation. "Seems like she deserved it, honestly. Like you both deserve it, fucking around with people's lives." And there's a glimmer in his eyes that sets me off—evil. Like he's enjoying this.

My breath catches in my throat, and suddenly all I can see is red. I reach for the nearest object to me—a shoe on the floor by the front door—and hurl it across the room, directly at Blaine's head.

All at once, voices spring to life, most directed at calming me down. Julian's hand is on my arm, preventing me from finding other things to throw. Sam seems to have settled back against a near wall, simply enjoying the show. Based on Blaine's tendency for girl drama, I wonder if this isn't that odd of an occurrence.

"You really are crazy," Blaine shouts, having dodged my assault.

"And you're an asshole," I shoot back.

"Vally, let's just go," Julian says.

"Yeah, listen to your boyfriend," Blaine snaps.

I'm grasping for something more to throw—shoes, words, insults—but Julian has already opened the front door and is pulling me out with him. He shuts it behind us and drags me across the lawn.

Once we reach the sidewalk, I yank my arm from his grip and simply walk angrily beside him. He acquiesces, content that I won't run back inside and launch myself at Blaine's neck. However badly I want to.

We walk in silence back to my car.

Chapter 12

Sitting in the dark car, Julian still not muttering a word, I can't help but feel disappointed. And stupid. And frustrated. Angry. Hopeless.

"You okay?" he asks softly.

And now I feel guilty. Because Julian should probably be mad at me. Furious. I shouldn't have dragged him into this. I shake my head. "No." And then I add, "I'm sorry. I shouldn't have asked you to come." I shoot him a guilty look. "I literally just sabotaged your whole day, and it turned into a literal nightmare." I start the car, the Beach Boys coming on again.

"No, Vally," Julian says. "It's okay. I mean . . . honestly, I'm glad I was there. It would've been dangerous to go alone."

He's just being nice. Nicer than I deserve.

I pull into the road, leaving Blaine's house behind. I open my mouth, but my protest dies on my tongue. What more can I say? Especially considering I'm still buzzing with adrenaline and anger right now. And I just can't stomach sitting around in my empty apartment without Brooklyn, knowing that she's . . .

I guess that's the problem. I don't know. I don't

know anything. And it's killing me. Confronting Blaine gave me absolutely no answers. The Beach Boys fill the silence around us, as I've become accustomed to them doing. Five minutes later, I park in the complex lot, and we hop out.

We walk in silence into the building. It reminds me of last night. The way we'd talked over dinner and then suddenly became awkward as we filed back to our respective homes. We reach our hallway and slowly come to a stop near our apartment doors.

"Are you going to be okay?" Julian asks again, looking down at his feet. Scuffed navy blue sneakers. He arranges his glasses on the bridge of his nose before looking up to meet my gaze.

I shrug. I don't have an answer. At least not one anybody would like. No. I'm not okay, and I'm not going to be okay. Not until Brooklyn comes home. Although, oddly, I feel like if I told him that, he wouldn't be uncomfortable. He probably already knows. He's looking at me like he knows. Those puppy dog eyes are back again.

"Do you have dinner in there?" He nods toward my apartment.

Only now do I realize that neither of us has eaten in hours. I think about it. I had the last noodle soup packet the other night, and I think the only other thing we have is an old head of broccoli. It's probably not even good anymore. I shrug.

Julian must know it's a lie because he pulls out his phone. "I'm ordering us food," he declares.

I stare at him in surprise. "You don't have to," I

protest. Especially after what I put him through tonight. "I'm not even hungry."

He grimaces. "Yeah, but that doesn't mean you can just not eat."

I stare at him as he pulls up some meal delivery service. He pauses, looks at me, then over my shoulder at the door to my apartment. He inclines his head in question.

I raise my eyebrows. "Okay," I mumble, pulling my keys from my pocket and making my way to the door.

Julian follows me inside, still scrolling through his phone. "What sounds good?" he asks as I shut the door behind him. "There's a Mexican place nearby that's open."

"Yeah, let's do that," I say. Nothing sounds good, so it really doesn't matter.

"Tacos?" he prompts again, probably reading my mind and knowing that everything would be equally unappetizing.

"Yeah."

He sits on the couch, finalizing the order, then sets his phone down and shoots me a triumphant smile. "They'll be here in twenty minutes."

I smile faintly. I'm still standing, just watching him. There are no other places to sit in here. No dining table, no chairs. Just the couch. After another awkward heartbeat, I force myself to take the spot on the opposite arm.

After a moment of silence, I say, "I don't know what else to do."

Julian sighs. He knows what I mean. I turn to see that expression back. Kindness, empathy, pity. Normally I hate that look. Pity. I like to smack it right off of people's faces. But for some reason, on Julian, it doesn't bother me so much. And deep down, I know he's right. It was a long shot. It was pretty amazing that I found Blaine's house in the first place. That we managed to get in. But what did I hope to find there other than a confrontation? I mentally kick myself. The idea was stupid.

But it doesn't deflate my suspicion. My brows knit together. Just because Brooklyn wasn't in the house doesn't mean he didn't kidnap her. Blaine might do nothing but deny it, but there is one other person who might be helpful. I pull up Instagram, scrolling through messages until I find hers. Katya. Blaine's girlfriend. Or ex-girlfriend. I'm honestly not even sure. The girl who hired me to catch him cheating.

"What are you doing?" Julian asks when he notices my attention shifting.

"I'm going to message someone," I answer.

```
Sarah: Hey. I have some questions
about Blaine. Can we talk ASAP?
```

It's blunt and a little demanding, but I don't care.

"I'm assuming this has something to do with Brooklyn," Julian states. He's become accustomed to fishing information out of me. I never really realized it until now, but I guess I'm not that forthright.

"It's Blaine's ex-girlfriend. She might be able to help."

Julian nods, biting the inside of his lip. "What if it isn't him?" he asks.

I shoot him a look. On what grounds is he making that claim? He knows nothing about the situation. About Brooklyn, about me, about Blaine. About the shit we get up to.

He must sense the shift because he backpedals a bit. "Just—are there other people you haven't considered? Why put all your focus on him?"

It's a good point. Honestly, Blaine was the first person that came to mind, and I've been latched on to the idea ever since. My saving grace. The one shred of hope that will bring Brooklyn home.

My phone buzzes, and my gaze shoots downward.

```
Katya: Uh, sure. What's this
about?
```

I grit my teeth, determining how to respond. I suppose I could just go all in. What's the use in beating around the bush? Hiding things.

```
Sarah: This is a little crazy,
but here goes. My roommate went
missing a few days ago. She's the
girl in the photos on the profile.
Right around the time she went
```

```
missing, Blaine started sending me
super harassing messages. I know
it's crazy, but is there any way he
could be involved?
```

"What are you asking her?" Julian says, leaning across the couch.

"I'm just trying to get her take on things. She knows him. I'm not even sure what I'm looking for, but I'll bet she has good insight."

Suddenly there's a knock on the door, and Julian hops to up to answer it. I'd almost forgotten about the food. He exchanges pleasantries, grabs the bag, and shuts the door. I sit, staring at my phone, waiting for a response, as Julian shuffles through the kitchen looking for plates and utensils. I don't bother helping. It's the size of a postage stamp—he'll find everything faster than I can help him.

He meanders back over with two plates full of tacos. He hands me one and then sits back down. Closer to me this time.

"Thank you." I stare down at the tacos on my plate. Beef, by the looks of them. Something I'd love to dig into any other time, but like the last few days, I'm still nauseous. But I should eat. Starving myself won't do anyone any good.

I set my phone aside, assuming Katya needs time to process my text.

I take one of the tacos in hand and take a small bite.

"Good?" Julian asks, eyebrows raised.

I shrug.

He laughs. "What do you normally eat?"

I shrug again. "I mean, I eat tacos a lot."

"So what's wrong with these ones?"

I smirk. "Nothing. These are great tacos, Julian. Thank you." I pause, the grin sliding just a bit. "Seriously. It's very nice of you to hang out with me." I shoot him a look. "I know what you're doing. You don't have to, though. I don't want to take up all your time."

His eyebrows furrow. "No. I mean, yeah, I am trying to take your mind off things. I know what it—well, I guess I don't know what it feels like. But I know it must be terrible. I'm not here just because of that, though. I'm here because . . ." He stares down at his half-eaten taco. "I like hanging out with you. I'm enjoying being here."

I raise my eyebrows at him. Really? He liked breaking into some random guy's house and starting an altercation? I smile at the absurdity of it. And I realize that I'm unexpectedly relieved. I didn't want him to hang around out of obligation, but the idea of him leaving sends a pang of loneliness through my chest. What would I do? Probably pace my apartment and obsessively blow up Katya's phone.

"Do you like vampires?" I ask.

Julian snorts. "No."

"Good. I've got a great show we can watch."

Chapter 13

"Do they have to make that face when using their powers?" Julian's mouth is pursed, trying to hold back a laugh.

"Yes, Julian," I say. "It's the way of the vampires."

His laugh bursts out. "Why do they even have powers, anyway? Isn't being a vampire power enough? Now they can wield fire and shit?"

I shoot him a pointed look. "If you knew more about vampires, you'd know that 'fire and shit' comes with the territory."

We finished our tacos long ago, and we're a few episodes in to the vampire show I've been binging the last few weeks. I've filled him in on pretty much everything he needed to know. Which honestly isn't much. And it's more fun to answer his questions and fill him in along the way.

"Oh, this one's a bitch," I tell him, pointing to the screen. "She slept with that one's boyfriend, but he didn't know it was her, so she blamed it on this other girl."

He frowns. "How did he not know it was her?"

"It was dark, and she was using some—magic thing."

"Magic thing?" he echoes.

"Yes, that's the technical term. Don't mock me."

"I have a question."

"Shoot."

"Okay." He repositions himself on the couch so he's facing me a bit more. His knee inches closer to mine, almost touching. "The vampires have the power to turn regular people into vampires, too, right?"

"Yes," I answer. "That's what recently happened to her." I point to a character on the screen.

"Right. So, if they have loved ones, they could just turn them and then live with them forever."

"Exactly."

"So." He leans forward. "What about dogs?" I open my mouth to reply, when he continues, "You can't leave man's best friend behind. What about your favorite pet? Can you bite them, too, and they'll live forever?" He leans back a bit, brows raised, point made.

I widen my eyes. "That is an excellent question."

He nods. "I know. Personally, I wouldn't want to be immortal if my dog couldn't be either."

I nod along.

"This is a huge worldbuilding flaw."

"I agree. We should take this up with the TV show creators," I suggest.

"It would give them limitless plotlines. Honestly, we'd deserve a cut."

I make a face. "We could be rich."

"We could drop out of college. Screw an education. We came up with vampire dogs."

"Vampire dogs," I echo. "Truly a goldmine."

He chuckles. I yawn, leaning back deeper into the cushions behind us. It's late. I know it's late, even though I've been avoiding checking the clock on my phone. Julian must know, too, but he doesn't say anything. Doesn't check the time, doesn't get up to leave.

The show continues and we watch in silence, making snide comments here and there.

"Who knew the life of a vampire was so sexy?" Julian asks.

"Everyone," I quip. "That's literally all vampires do, is have sex. All day. With a million different people."

I keep waiting for my phone to buzz, for Katya to respond. But it's been hours now, and she hasn't. Either she'll reply tomorrow or she'll never reply at all. In which case, I'll find her just like I found Blaine. I'm not worried about that. She'll talk to me.

I can tell Julian is losing steam by the way his eyelids keep drooping. The kind part of me wants to suggest that he go home, get some rest, but the selfish part of me wants him here. He's the only thing distracting me from a total meltdown.

And I think he knows that.

Sweet man. Caring, adorable, sweet man. What the hell is he doing here? Caring about *me*? I'm the last person anyone should be caring for.

I don't remember falling asleep. I guess no one ever really does. It's just strange when you do it in such an unusual place. As if you should remember every second of it.

I wake to sunlight streaming in from the window above me. Above the couch. The TV must have automatically paused, because the show has stopped.

It takes me a minute to remember what the hell I was doing. Why I'm in the living room, lying on the couch . . . with another person.

With a jolt, I realize the warmth underneath me is not just from me, not from my heating pad or any other reasonable explanation—but from a whole other person.

I shift, realizing that my head is in Julian's lap while he is leaning over the armrest, fast asleep. I freeze. My head rests on his thigh, my hand on his knee. How did I end up falling asleep like this? Did I fall asleep first? What the actual hell?

I scooch my feet underneath me, trying to move as slowly as possible so as not to wake Julian. But just as I'm about to lift my head, he shifts. I hear him inhale, and suddenly I'm looking up into his dark eyes.

"Hey," he says, his voice groggy and cracking.

"Good morning," I say quietly. "Sorry." I scramble up from his lap so fast that blood rushes to my head and I need to steady myself on the couch. My back aches from the sudden movement—and from spending the night curled up on a couch. I wince.

"No, it's okay," he responds quickly.

"I didn't—" I start. "Did I fall asleep first?"

He makes a face. "Honestly, I don't remember. That show was too engaging." He smirks, the awkwardness fading. I grin back.

"Do you want coffee or something?" I stand, making my way to the small kitchen. Regardless of his answer, I want coffee, so I start making a pot.

"Sure, that would be great."

I start pouring water into the receptacle. I glance at the clock on the wall above the fridge. It's about 9 a.m. "Do you have, like, a job or something?" I ask, suddenly aware that I've kept him here way too long. I feel bad. Julian must have some sort of life. Obligations. And here I am keeping him away from all of that.

"No, actually," he calls back. "I have an on-campus job during the school year, but since school's out, I don't really have anything to do. I've applied at a few places, but no bites yet."

"Oh." Reasonable. I feel a little less guilty.

While the coffee is brewing, I go back and sit on the couch. Julian's glasses are perched on the side table, and his hair is slightly askew. He still looks sleepy. I probably do too.

"You know," I begin. "You don't have to do this."

He frowns slightly. "Do what?"

I exhale, gesturing aimlessly. "What you're doing. I don't know . . . comforting me. Staying with me." I shoot him a meaningful look. "I appreciate it, I really do." I look down at the sofa, at the foot of space between us. "But I don't want to keep you from—"

"You're not keeping me from anything."

I look up. He seems serious. Genuine. I tilt my head in question.

And suddenly he's reached out and grasped my hand between his fingers. "I care. About you. About Brooklyn. I want to be here for you. Someone needs to."

My frown deepens. "But you don't know me. Or her."

He shrugs. "It doesn't mean I can't care." Then he smiles. "Besides, I know you now. At least a little, right?"

I suppose that's true. We did just spend pretty much the entirety of the last forty-eight hours together. Doing weird shit, too. Stalking some random guy, discussing vampire lore.

Even while most of me might want to fight this, send him home, a tiny part of me wants to give in. Let him be there. Let him help. And deep down, I know that being alone right now is probably the worst thing I could do—even if it's what I might naturally crave. I have this idea that I'd get more done, that I'd become some superhuman detective and solve Brooklyn's disappearance, when in actuality I'd probably end up metaphorically setting myself on fire and imploding. Metaphors aside, I might actually burn something down. And it might be Blaine's fucking house.

No, it's a good thing Julian is here. At the very least to keep me from going to jail for arson.

My coffee pot beeps, and I gently pull my fingers from Julian's grasp. He seems suddenly embarrassed, like he hadn't meant to touch me.

I come back with two cups, handing one to Julian. He smiles in thanks and blows over the steaming mug. "Did you ever get a response from Katya?"

Adrenaline shoots through me. Katya. I'd completely forgotten. What the hell is wrong with me? I nearly spill my coffee, searching around the couch for my phone. Julian leans forward, taking the cup from my hands. I reach into the cushions, finding my phone buried beneath. I open the app, and her response blinks up at me.

```
Katya: Wow. I'm so sorry. That is
crazy. Honestly, I doubt Blaine
would have done anything, though.
```

Hm. It's not an unexpected response by any means. Of course she would say that. Or maybe not. If she truly hated him enough, she might say anything. But calling your ex a jackass and accusing him of kidnapping are two very different things. She might be genuine. I just don't know.

```
Sarah: Are you guys still
together? Has he been acting weird
the last few days?
```

I'm not ready to let this go.

"What's she saying?" Julian asks from beside me.

"She says he probably doesn't have anything to do with it."

He shrugs. "Typical."

I glance at him. "I know, that's what I think too."

Suddenly my phone buzzes not once, but continuously. Startled, I look down to see an incoming Instagram call. From Katya. Shit. Julian and I stare at each other wide-eyed.

"Answer it!" he says, and before I lose my nerve, I do exactly that.

"Hi, Katya," I say.

"Hi." She sounds hesitant.

"I'm so sorry that this is so out of the blue and weird," I begin. "But I need to find my roommate." I allow my voice to sound pleading, to show her how worried I am. There's nothing to lose at this point. I've already lost Brooklyn.

She sighs. "I know. I truly understand."

"Are you and Blaine still together?"

A heavier sigh. "It's complicated. We just started talking again."

In any other circumstance, I'd tell her to ditch his ass. He's obviously a jerk, what the hell is she doing back with him? But I bite my tongue. It doesn't matter. Brooklyn is what matters. "So, you've been around him more?" I prompt.

"Yeah."

"Have you noticed anything weird?"

"Nothing out of the ordinary. And honestly, he just wouldn't do something like that." But that's what anyone would say. It *is* what people say. I've watched enough of those true-crime documentaries to know that every neighbor, every friend will swear up and down that *Billy was a* nice *person. He'd never do anything bad. He'd surely never kill anyone.*

"He started bombarding me with messages," I tell her. "Like, threatening."

There's a pause on the other end of the line. "He might be a jerk," she says slowly, "but he's also an idiot."

I raise my eyebrows.

"He's not . . . *capable* of that. And I don't mean that in a moral way. I mean, obviously he should be morally above that but—logistically, he wouldn't be able to." She laughs humorlessly. "He couldn't pull anything like that off. He just couldn't."

I feel like I've been hit in the chest by a ton of bricks. Because I feel the sincerity in her voice. Regardless of whether it's true, Katya fully believes it.

"Thank you," I eventually say.

"Yeah." There's a heartbeat of silence. "I hope you find her."

When I end the call, Julian is watching me expectantly. I shake my head, tossing my phone to the cushion beside me. "She says he wouldn't do it."

He nods, gaze still glued to mine. "And what do you think?"

"She believes it." I pause for a moment, sucking in a breath. "But I don't."

Chapter 14

Blaine may be a hardened jerk—a kidnapper—but I doubt he's psychopathic. He probably kidnapped Brooklyn on a whim, blinded by rage and arrogance. Basically, where a true sociopath might be able to pull off the perfect crime, I know there are cracks in Blaine's armor. So, I'm going to find them.

And I'm going to do it by pressuring him until he cracks. At the very least, his life is going to become a living hell.

I wait for Julian to go back to his apartment to shower, then I head out. Based on his hesitancy last night—albeit justified—he's not going to like what I have planned next. Maybe I'll fill him in later, but I don't need him holding me back. Besides, it's the middle of the day, and where I'm going is a public place. I don't need protection.

Through a more thorough stalking of Blaine's Facebook page, I've found out he works at a bank downtown. Probably as an office assistant or intern.

My car putters its way to downtown Ozona—if you could even call it a downtown. It's a couple blocks on one street where most of the businesses are gathered. I park as close as I can to the bank and hop out of the car.

I'm a little jittery as I stride down the sidewalk. Kind of like the time I stood up for Brooklyn back in freshman year—to the girl who'd called her names. Kind of like the time I confronted Matt for cheating on me. Kind of like every time I'm about to stir shit up.

And damn am I about to stir some shit.

A bell above the door dings as my feet hit the carpeted floor. I glance around. It's a decent-sized bank. About six reception stations are stretched out across a long counter-like desk that spans the length of the room. To my right is a sitting area with couches and a coffee stand. To my left is a hallway with glass-walled offices. There's a handful of people currently being served, so I'm not immediately conspicuous.

With a jolt of satisfaction, I spot Blaine in a corner behind the reception stand, sitting at a computer.

I make a beeline toward him, past the couches, past the handful of people chatting away with their respective bank tellers. I reach the long wall of desks, and the teller nearest me shoots me a glance.

I'm only about five feet away from Blaine, but his back is turned—he hasn't seen me yet. I rest my elbows on the desk, leaning forward. "Blaine?" I call. It's a tone I rarely use. It's sweet, nice, friendly.

He turns at the sound, and then his gaze rests on me. A series of emotions flickers across his face. Surprise, confusion, concern, suspicion. "You," he utters quietly.

I can't suppress the snort.

He abruptly stands, shooting a nervous glance toward the row of bank tellers. "What are you doing here?" he hisses.

I shrug. "Our conversation last night wasn't as productive as I would have liked. I wanted to continue it."

He narrows his eyes. "Look. Like I said, I don't know anything about your friend, or—anything! Just get out of here."

I feign an expression of sympathy. "Hm. Blaine, that's not a very nice way to treat a customer," I say.

His gaze hardens. His jaw clenches. He takes a small step toward the desk, but I don't back up. "Get the fuck out," he warns, soft enough for no one else to hear.

I purse my lips, glancing to my left. People have noticed our conversation. From our body language, I'm sure they're getting a very distinct vibe. One of the tellers in particular is outright staring. I look back to Blaine. "Just tell me where Brooklyn is, and I'll leave." I smile.

"That's your problem, not mine," he spits.

My smile drops, and I straighten. Fine. Fucker. "Come on. You're gonna regret not just telling me."

Blaine leans forward on the desk, barely a foot from my face. "What is your problem? I have nothing to do with whatever you think is happening," he mutters. "What are you going to do? Cause a scene?"

I shrug. "I don't know. Maybe."

His expression pales a bit at that.

I grin. But no. Causing a disruption and ruining every other employee's day here isn't what I'm here for. Besides, it's not enough—Blaine deserves more than just minor embarrassment.

I shove back from the counter. "No worries, Blaine. I'm sure I'll be seeing you later."

His expression melts into one of confusion as I turn on my heels and exit the bank.

It wasn't exactly an unexpected outcome—although I would have preferred it if he'd just told me where the fuck Brooklyn is. The thought causes me to clench my teeth together.

I reach my car, open the passenger's-side door, and pull a screwdriver out of the glove compartment. I know he drives an old silver truck, and I wrote his license plate number down after seeing him pull into his driveway yesterday. And if he's at work, the truck is somewhere nearby.

It only takes about five minutes to locate it—parked in a lot behind the bank building used mostly by downtown business employees. There are no cameras that I can see—and honestly, at this point, would I care if there were?—or windows facing the parking lot. I glance around to make sure I'm alone, then jam the screwdriver into his right front tire.

It pops and hisses, slowly sinking. I make my way around the car, stabbing each tire as I go, until the truck is a flat, sad mess.

This, for sure, will piss him off. And I'm nowhere near done.

Chapter 15

I don't go home. Instead, I drive through McDonald's, grab a hamburger and fries, and park myself outside Blaine's house. I don't know when he gets off work, but I'm not going to take the chance of missing him.

In the meantime, I plan my next avenue of attack. But who knows if I'll have to employ it? We'll see how he's feeling when he gets home from work. He's either going to be pissed—most likely—or he'll be scared straight enough to tell me where Brooklyn is. I'm hoping for the latter but prepared for the former.

A few hours later, a different car eventually pulls into the driveway. I'm assuming he had to get his truck towed. He hops out and, to my surprise, so does Katya. So, they *are* dating again. Or at least, he was able to bum a ride from her. I frown. It's a shame. She really does deserve better. Or, more accurately, he does not deserve—well, anyone. Kidnapping aside, he's a complete jackass.

I'm parked much closer to the house this time. Close enough that Blaine catches a glimpse of me through the windshield—which I'd expected.

I smile and wave.

Even from fifteen feet away, I can see the murder in his eyes. He says something to Katya and stalks toward my car. I roll my window down just a few inches. Don't want him lunging inside.

"You fucking bitch!" he spits, banging his fist against my door.

"Great way to start a conversation, Blaine," I snap back at him.

"You're crazy—I knew it was you!" he shouts, clenching his fists. He looks like he's about to hit my car again when Katya grabs him by the arm. He roughly pushes her off. "You're crazy," he repeats, leveling me with an incredulous stare. As if this insult should far outweigh any others. As if crazy just materializes. As if crazy isn't cultivated by men just like him. I'll bet he called Katya crazy when she accused him of cheating.

"You can end this," I remind him calmly. "All I need is Brooklyn."

"I don't know shit about your stupid friend!"

"Really?" I counter. "Because your most recent messages to Sarah imply otherwise." I pull out my phone, reading from our Instagram chat. "'Watch your back. I'm gonna fuck you up'? What do you think the police would think of that?" I leave out the fact that the police already have access to the account, and would most likely know about the messages if they'd done their due diligence—and don't seem to fucking care, apparently. But Blaine doesn't need to know that.

At this, Blaine's face drains of all aggression, and for the first time, he actually looks scared. His mouth drops open, and his brows furrow together. He shakes his head. "Look. I was just pissed. I didn't mean anything by those messages, honestly. I have no idea what happened to your friend." He takes a small step away from my car, assuming a less threatening pose.

Katya is furiously glancing between us, gleaning pieces of the story that she's missed. She whirls on me. "Blaine wouldn't kidnap your friend," she defends him. "I told you that!"

"I'm not convinced yet."

"Well, too bad!" she says, angry now. "I'm sorry about your friend, but leave us alone." She yanks on Blaine's jacket, and after shooting me another dirty look, he reluctantly follows her back to the house.

I watch them vanish inside, and I bite my lip in thought. The fear I saw in Blaine's eyes looked real. Very real. The idea of involving the police truly scared him. But what is he scared of? Being falsely accused of a crime, or of actually paying the consequences of his actions?

I click my jaw, staring at the house. It's him. It has to be him, no matter how hard he denies it. He sends threatening messages to Sarah's Instagram account, and the next day Brooklyn goes missing? It's not a coincidence.

I stare down at the screenshots on my phone that I've been compiling all afternoon while waiting in the car. Screenshots of every disgusting, horrible, sexist thing he's ever messaged me. All the gross pickup lines. The incriminating messages I'd sent Katya to prove he was cheating. The unsolicited dick pic. And the threatening messages from a few days ago.

And then there's his Facebook friends list. The one with his buddies, family, professors, acquaintances. Because if you truly believe the shit you say, why be ashamed if everyone sees it? I'm sure not.

I begin compiling the mass messenger list, attaching the photos to my draft one by one. I'm typing up some kind of message, tagging Blaine's profile, when a car pulls into the driveway.

At first, I assume it must be Sam, but a girl gets out. I watch her walk up to the door, pull out a key, and walk in. Sam's girlfriend perhaps? I didn't see one in the very thorough stalking I did of his page in order to find their address—but that doesn't necessarily mean he doesn't have one.

Then I hear shouting. I sit up in my seat and lean over the steering wheel, eyes glued to the window, even though there's a curtain and I can't see anything. The shouting continues, although I can't make it out.

Suddenly Katya emerges from the front door, slamming it shut behind her. She storms down the driveway and up to her car.

I throw my door open and jog down the

pavement before she has a chance to drive off. "Katya!" I call, running up to her window. She turns, sees me, and then rolls her eyes. "What happened?" I call through the window, gesturing for her to roll it down.

She shakes her head, obviously still annoyed with me. But she seems torn. The window rolls down. "He's a piece of shit, that's what happened," she snaps at me.

It doesn't take a genius to put the pieces together. "He was cheating with that girl?" I ask.

She snorts. "What, do you know about that too?"

"I just assumed."

She shakes her head again, wiping at tears that are about to fall. "God, I'm so stupid. He does this over and over again. What am I thinking?"

I purse my lips. Yeah. What *was* she thinking? But at the same time, almost all of us have been there. I certainly have. Matt shattered my heart into a million pieces, and I still wanted him back. It's some stupid, terrible curse, I guess.

"I'm sorry," I offer. And I mean it.

She sniffs, and for a second, I think she's going to yell at me again. But then she nods. "Yeah. Thanks."

I watch her back out of the driveway and drive off, her words from our earlier phone conversation ringing through my head. *He's not capable.*

I think of the guy who clumsily cheated on his girlfriend. The guy who left his back door unlocked. The guy who sent stupidly incriminating text messages and photos. The guy who gave *two separate girls* the keys to his house.

It's slowly sinking in, however hard I want to ignore it. That Blaine truly might not be capable of kidnapping Brooklyn. At least not successfully. For God's sake, he can't even cheat without getting caught.

I get back in my car and sit in silence. I open my phone back up and stare at the message I'd been drafting. My conviction of him being a kidnapper is slowly fading. But the look in Katya's eyes as she drove off reignites the vigilante inside me. Her face as she rushed out of that house. Not to mention all the gross stuff he's said to me.

He may not be a kidnapper, but he's still an asshole.

So I press send.

Chapter 16

I spend the night tossing and turning, and by morning I'm about to have a mental breakdown. Because Blaine was my only lead, and by letting go of him, I'm letting go of the one ounce of control I had over this situation.

I shower, hoping it will calm me down and help me think, but it doesn't. I decide to make coffee, even though I know it will most likely only hype me up. The ritual itself is a distraction.

There's a knock on my door, and for a moment I think it might be the police. Maybe they have more information, maybe they have good news. But when I open it, Julian stands on the threshold.

"Hi," I greet, letting him inside.

"Hey," he says. "Where'd you go yesterday? I came back, but you were gone."

I shrug, walking back to my coffee maker. "You probably won't like the answer."

He follows me, and when I turn around, he's making that same worried face from the other night. Somehow both his eyebrows and his nose are scrunched up. "What does that mean?"

"It means you're probably going to tell me it was a bad idea."

"Well, was it?"

I shoot him a deadpan look, then shake my head. "I don't know."

"So, what'd you do?"

I grab a bright-pink coffee mug from the shelf above me and start pouring coffee. "I threatened Blaine at his workplace and slashed his tires. Then I sat outside his house for a few hours until he came home, and he yelled at me. I also sent his dick pic to everyone on his Facebook friends list."

I hold my mug up, blowing before taking a sip. I meet Julian's gaze over the dark liquid. The scrunch in his brow is gone, replaced by wide eyes. He almost looks scared.

Good. He *should* be afraid of me.

But that fear quickly vanishes, replaced by simple surprise. He purses his lips, nodding slowly. "Okay." He watches me calmly as I take another sip of coffee. "How are you feeling?"

I frown at him. That's a stupid question. Completely beside the point. What does he mean, how do I feel? I feel awful. Brooklyn is still missing. I sigh angrily.

"I don't think it's Blaine."

He nods again, and I can't tell if his calm demeanor is comforting or maddening.

"It's not him," I repeat, my voice hitching a bit this time.

He continues to watch me, stiff.

I shake my head, panic starting to swirl in. Because when I had a suspect, when I had a mission, a reason, hope that I could find Brooklyn, I was able to push it aside. I was able to ignore my fear, assume it was all misguided. But now there's nothing. Nothing but the dread taking hold in my veins.

Because it's not Blaine. It's not him. But there are dozens of Blaines. Men whose lives I've ruined under Brooklyn's guise. Men who hate her, blame her, want her dead. And it's all my fault.

Suddenly my hands are shaking, and I smack the mug down on the counter to keep from dropping it. Coffee spills out onto the tile. I suck in a huge breath, my hands clenching the edge of the countertop.

I lean forward, and suddenly I'm just imploding, huddled on the floor with my back against the cupboard doors.

"It's my fault," I whisper, my hands pressed to my cheeks. I pull my knees up to my chest, leaning into myself. Fuck. What was I thinking? What the hell was I thinking doing this? Angering strange men I don't even know. Men who think it's *Brooklyn* who's fucking with their lives. Brooklyn who would never hurt a fly. Perfect, beautiful Brooklyn. And I've done this to her.

I don't realize I'm hyperventilating until Julian has kneeled before me, grabbed ahold of both my wrists, and is mere inches from my face. "Vally," he says. He sounds worried, scared. "It's okay. It's okay."

"No, it's not okay!" I yank away from him, immediately guilty when I see the look on his face.

"Brooklyn is *missing*, and I don't know where she is. I don't know how to fix it."

He stares at me, helpless. "I . . ."

I make some sort of strange, anguished sound I've never heard myself make before.

"It's not your fault." But those words feel empty. He can't say that. He doesn't know. He doesn't know how truly guilty I am.

He reaches for me again, grasping my hand in his. It's all he can really do, and I let him.

"I need to find her. I need to fix this," I murmur.

"You can't fix it, Vally," he tells me. He takes a breath as if wanting to say more, but strangles on the words.

"You don't understand." And this is where my resolve breaks. Where my hesitancy collapses and flows away. Because why am I even hiding anymore? Who cares if everyone knows how terrible of a person I am? All I care about is getting Brooklyn back. And in this moment, if I don't keep talking, spilling my guts, I might just sob myself into oblivion. "I suspected Blaine because he knew us. Well, Sarah—Brooklyn." I shake my head. "What matters is that he thinks Brooklyn did something horrible to him. But she didn't. I did." And I spill. And spill and spill and spill. "We run this Instagram account. Her name is Sarah, but she's Brooklyn's photos, and I manage it. We use it to bait guys into cheating on their girlfriends. Girlfriends who reach out to us and ask us to, but we do it. Then we send them the screenshots to prove it. To show their boyfriends how fucked up they are."

Julian is still holding my hand. He hasn't pulled away. I glance up, expecting to see all compassion, kindness, caring gone, replaced by revulsion. Or at least concern. But surprisingly, his expression doesn't change one bit. He just stares back at me, taking it in, letting me speak.

"The guys think they're talking to Brooklyn, even if they don't know her real name. So, when Blaine reached out to the page again, calling me names, threatening me . . . and then she went missing . . ."

"You assumed the worst," Julian fills in.

I nod, a sob gurgling up my throat. "But it's worse now," I say. "Because if it wasn't Blaine . . . Fuck, Julian. There are so many of them."

His expression does change now. Deeper. Fearful. He understands. He truly gets it now. "You think it's one of the guys you catfished?"

"It has to be. Who else would want to hurt her?"

I can feel another bubble of panic threatening to escape. I clench Julian's hand. It's the only thing I have. I squeeze my eyes closed and take a shuddering breath, praying the flood will stop. I can't save Brooklyn if I'm a fucking mess.

Get it together, Valerie.

"Hey, hey." Julian's hand lets mine go, and suddenly both are cupping my face. "Vally," he breathes, and my eyes open. He's close to me, so close.

"I will help you find Brooklyn," he states. "We'll find her."

I'm nodding, staring into his eyes, losing myself in the feel of his fingertips against my cheeks. Warm and rough at the same time. My breathing has calmed, has slowly evened—but now is affected by something else entirely. Some strange electricity that wasn't here before, but most certainly is now.

Just then, my eye snags on the kitchen wall behind him. At the clock. "Oh, shit." I scramble up, Julian's arms falling to his sides. "I have work today."

"Oh." He stands, following my gaze to the clock.

"Shit," I say again, jogging to my room and hastily pulling out my work uniform.

"Can I help you? Do you need a ride?" Julian calls from the kitchen. It's sweet, even though he knows I have my own car. What good would driving me do? I suppose he just wants to feel useful. Is probably wondering whether I'm mentally stable enough considering the meltdown I just had.

"No, no, I'm good." I run a comb through my hair and pull it up into a ponytail. No time for makeup, not that I normally wear a whole lot of it anyway. "You can have some coffee," I tell Julian, reappearing from my room and motioning toward the full coffeemaker. "Or take some with you—or whatever."

He's nodding. "Yeah, okay."

"Yeah." We're standing so close that I think he might touch me again. But the moment is strange and weird and filled with an energy I don't quite understand. "Okay." I grab my keys and purse off the side table, and Julian follows me out the door.

"I'll see you later?" I ask.

Julian smiles. "Knock on my door when you get off work."

Chapter 17

Much like the day before, my shift at the smoothie shop is practically the seventh circle of hell. All I can think about is getting back home and stalking the fuck out of every man who's ever come into contact with Sarah's account. It's the only lead I have. I spend my brief moments of downtime gathering a list of names based on the account's message history. Starting with guys who were vocally unhappy about our meddling. Not quite as violent-sounding as Blaine, but close enough.

When a coworker comes to relieve my shift, I basically sprint out the door. I reach the apartment complex and park in the lot, wondering if Julian was serious about me knocking on his door when I got home. We did just spend the last few days together. But maybe he's sick of me and needs time to focus on something other than finding his neighbor's roommate. And then there was the total breakdown I had this morning. And the feel of his hands against my face, my neck . . .

Aside from murderous thoughts about Brooklyn's kidnapper, Julian has weirdly taken center stage in my mind for the day. Which I feel guilty as fuck about.

Brooklyn. That's all I should be focusing on. Getting her back. And I am. I just happened to also have some weird encounter with Julian Sun, and now my mind has been turned to mush.

But then I practically ran out of the apartment to go to work. Was that . . . weird? Was he about to kiss me, but I literally ran away? God. Maybe knocking on his door wouldn't be such a great idea after all.

I run my hands down my face, sighing. The one time I have any kind of romantic connection with someone, it happens during the middle of a literal crisis. Perfect.

I hop out of my car, locking it behind me. I spy Brooklyn's car in the corner, where it hasn't moved for days. A sick feeling takes hold of my gut. I take a deep breath and keep walking.

Suddenly a voice rings out across the parking lot, and I groan internally.

"Vally!" I hear the footsteps scampering up behind me, and I don't need to turn to know who it is.

"Hey, Sylvie."

"Heyyy." The word is drawn out—much like the way she speaks when she and Brooklyn are engaging in gossip. Except I'll bet anything that Brooklyn herself is going to be the topic of this conversation. She steps in front of me, halting my path toward the building. Her eyes are wide, and she leans in conspiratorially. "Where the hell is Brooklyn?"

I grimace. That's the million-dollar question. I open my mouth to supply some kind of answer, but Sylvie keeps going.

"We were supposed to meet up yesterday, but she never showed. And she's not answering my texts. Then I remembered that weird thing *you* texted me the other day. So, I texted you. But you didn't respond." She looks at me expectantly.

Oh. Shit. Yeah, I guess I had seen some texts from Sylvie come through. My grimace deepens. "Sorry. I've been preoccupied."

"Well, at least you guys weren't kidnapped," she says with a laugh, gesturing to my obviously-not-kidnapped form.

Oof. I open my mouth again, but nothing comes out. Because what the hell am I supposed to say? Ugh. I was hoping to keep Sylvie out of this. I suppose she does deserve to know—she's Brooklyn's friend too. But deep down, I'd been hoping we'd find her sooner than this. That there wouldn't be anything to tell other than some story about how Brooklyn *safely* survived a kidnapping. And then it'd be Brooklyn telling the story, not me.

But now it's been four days, a number I don't even want to think about, because if I think about it for too long—

"Oh my God." Noticing my lack of response to her joke, she's now staring me down. I haven't said anything yet, but I know she can read it in my eyes. "Is Brooklyn okay? Where is she?"

Again with that fucking question. "I don't know

where she is. Nobody does." It's such a defeat to say it out loud, and it's only made worse by the way Sylvie leaps forward, clinging to me, her nails digging into the flesh on my arms.

"You're not serious," she demands.

"I'm not joking."

"What . . ." She trails off, speechless. A first for her.

I brush past her, tired of standing in the hot sun. And honestly, I don't have the emotional capacity to comfort a distraught Sylvie. I barely have the emotional capacity to be around her when she's happy. I'll try to respond to her texts and update her if anything happens. That's the best I can do. And it's what Brooklyn would want anyway.

God. What the hell am I doing talking about her as if she's dead? She's not dead.

Sylvie rushes after me, peppering me with questions. "Did you call the police?"

"Yeah."

"Is there footage from the apartment complex?"

"The police investigated; there's nothing useful." I reach the sidewalk, nearing the front doors.

"What about her dashcam?"

I halt, my purse jingling as it collides with my side. I glance back. "Her what?" But I already know the answer. The memories are falling back into place. The dashcam Brooklyn bought a few months back after a handful of cars were broken into in our apartment complex. My heartrate increases.

"The dashcam in her car," Sylvie repeats.

All other thoughts abandoned, I rush back into the parking lot, making my way across the asphalt, Sylvie on my heels. Brooklyn's car is still parked in the corner. The sick feeling in my stomach from earlier intensifies the closer I get. I don't know what it is about her car, but I hate looking at it. A reminder that she abandoned it. That she's gone. That she's *been* gone for days. But I push through it and walk up to the passenger's-side door. I lean over and peer inside.

My heartbeat spikes. There it is. The dashcam.

Sylvie and I turn to look at each other, each just as shocked.

I instinctively try the door handle, but it's locked. And who knows where her keys are? With her, most likely. Sylvie tries all the other doors, but to no avail.

"Should we somehow break in?" Sylvie suggests. "It's not a crime if we're trying to save our friend, right?"

Who fucking cares if it's a crime? I'm only worried about the logistics of it. How hard is it to break a car window? Would ramming it with my own car be worthwhile? Probably not.

But maybe I don't need the actual camera. Didn't she say something about some software she installed? I lean closer, reading the brand name on the side. *Milton*.

"We don't need to get inside," I tell Sylvie, beckoning her to follow me. And then I'm running across the parking lot, up the stairs, through the hallway, and into my apartment. Sylvie rushes in after me, breathless. I toss my purse and keys on the couch, heading for Brooklyn's room.

I'm accosted with the smell of her perfume. She's worn the same scent since freshman year. Her bed is unmade, her covers rumpled like they always are. I scan the room, searching for a laptop, praying that she didn't have it with her. But why would she? School isn't in session, there's no reason she would have been carrying it around with her.

The desk is empty, so I scan the floor. And there it is. Plugged in, sitting on the rug beside her bed. I sink to my knees, pulling it open. There's no password, thank God. She never really saw the need for one. *Who would want to break into my laptop? There's nothing on there.*

We all say that about being kidnapped, too, and look where that got us.

Sylvie follows me in and perches on the bed above me, hovering over my shoulder, watching the screen.

I type *Milton* into the search bar at the bottom of the screen and wait while it loads. A few seconds later, there it is. Milton Security Camera. I open the program. A list of dates sprawls out before me. When was it?

Today is Thursday. Brooklyn's been gone for four days. The number hits me like a punch to the stomach. Four whole days. I shake my head, counting backward. She went missing on Sunday June 13th.

I click the date, and it pulls up dozens of footage options. They look like they're separated by half-hour increments. I scan the times. The last time I saw her was in the smoothie shop. What time did she come by? I try to remember my shift that day. It was the afternoon.

I decide to ignore any footage before twelve p.m. And I begin. I click on the first video, scrubbing through the footage with my mouse. The car is driving. It parks on the street near my work. This must be when she came by to see me. The next video shows the car leaving, ending up at the grocery store we frequent. It ends right as the car starts again.

"How many of these are there?" Sylvia asks. I ignore her question.

I click the next video, my adrenaline getting out of hand. This has to be it. The car made it back to the apartment, and that's exactly where she would have been heading after getting groceries.

The footage shows the car entering the parking lot, making its way over to the corner where she normally parks. Where the car is parked right now. I feel sick to my stomach. My heart is thrumming in my ears.

The camera is pointing out the front window, so I can't tell what Brooklyn is doing. Most likely getting out of the car by the way the frame shakes slightly.

Suddenly there's another car. It comes out of nowhere, parking in front of hers, blocking her in. Someone jumps out, but I can't quite make out his features. The quality isn't good, the window is dirty. He also has . . . something on his head? His face?

Is that a fucking ski mask?

Sylvia gasps from above me, and the bed creaks as she leans back, away from the screen.

The figure runs to the driver's side of Brooklyn's car and disappears for a few seconds.

And then my stomach drops. He comes back into frame, dragging a struggling Brooklyn, his hand over her mouth. She claws at his arms, reaches for his face, but he's strong and he holds her down.

My hands go to my mouth, and I lean back on my heels. Some strange sound between a scream and a sob escapes my throat. I want to squeeze my eyes shut, but I can't. I can't. I have to watch this. It takes a few minutes, but Brooklyn eventually goes limp, and he drags her the few feet to his car, hoisting her into the backseat. He jumps into the driver's seat, and the car takes off. I replay the last few seconds, praying I'll get a glimpse of the license plate, but the angle is off, and there are things in the way.

I stop the video, sitting in stunned silence. Sylvie is shrieking something unintelligible at me, grabbing my shoulders, but I'm unable to process her. Anything she's saying, doing—anything at all. Because shit just got real. Up until now, I could still hold out hope that Brooklyn was okay. That there was some stupid explanation for this. That she went home to visit family without telling me. That she was being selfish and just a bad friend. I wish more than anything that she was nothing more than just a bad friend right now. A bad friend who's alive and safe and happy.

Adrenaline is still coursing through me, setting my veins on fire, blowing up my brain. But it's beginning to change now. From fear and desperation to anger. Furious, righteous anger. I dig my fingernails into my palms, glaring at the screen.

And any awkwardness I'd felt earlier about seeing Julian again vanishes. He said he'd help me find Brooklyn, and I'm going to hold him to that.

Because I'm going to find whoever this motherfucker is and end him.

Chapter 18

Julian opens the door with a smile that immediately falters when he sees my face. "Bad day at work?" he asks hollowly, and then his gaze slides past me to where I know Sylvie is standing. "Oh. Hi."

"Julian, this is Sylvie, Brooklyn's friend. Sylvie, this is Julian."

He smiles faintly.

"Brooklyn's been kidnapped, and we have proof!" Sylvie exclaims from behind me.

"He knows," I tell her. "Well, not about the proof." I look back to him, gesturing to the laptop tucked under my arm.

His eyes widen, and he takes a step back, ushering us into his apartment. It's the first time I've been in here. It's the same layout as mine, which is weird to see. It's basically my apartment but . . . guy themed. There are no decorations. Just an old couch, a TV on the floor, and piles of dishes in the sink. I see video game controllers piled in the corner. I remember him talking about *The Sims* when we first went out to dinner. I wonder if him roommate plays too.

"I'm assuming the proof has something to do with the laptop?" he asks, shutting the door.

I spin around. "It's Brooklyn's laptop. She has a dashcam in her car, and the footage shows her being kidnapped." The statement feels like both an accomplishment and a desperate loss. We have proof of what happened. What should never have happened in the first place.

Julian pales. "Can you see who it was?"

I roll my eyes, shaking my head. "He was wearing some sort of mask. Meaning he obviously planned this. And I couldn't make out the license plate on his car. But it's certain now. She was kidnapped."

Julian takes a deep breath. "Okay." He pauses for a moment. "Wow."

I nod, taking a seat on the couch and opening the laptop. I pull up the incriminating footage, but don't play it. I don't need to see Brooklyn struggling again. The initial sight of it made me want to vomit. Sylvie sits quietly next to me. It's the longest I've ever seen her go without talking. "We need to send this to the police."

He nods, eyebrows furrowed. "Maybe now they'll listen."

I agree. "This proves that it's serious. I know they thought she was just some dumb college kid who ran away for the weekend. This will show them that's not true."

My comment brings forth a shocked look from Sylvie. "Seriously?" she asks.

I nod, searching for the email address the officers

had me send Brooklyn's pictures to. I find it in my sent inbox on my phone. I pull up the footage on the laptop and send it to the same address with a reminder of who I am, what the situation is, and how I found the footage. Sylvie watches over my shoulder. I lean back with a sigh, feeling less accomplished than I thought I would.

Because, ultimately, what if the police still don't care? This won't necessarily find Brooklyn right away. They probably won't even get to the video until tomorrow. It's already late in the day. And they haven't been at all attentive up to this point.

"What do we do now?" Sylvie asks.

I heave an audible sigh, but then immediately feel bad upon seeing Sylvie's face. It's not her fault I'm completely and utterly drained and the idea of holding her hand through this is too exhausting for me to bear. "Honestly," I begin. "We just wait."

"Wait?" she echoes. "We can't just wait. The police need to view the footage now so they can find Brooklyn."

I nod along. "I know, but they've been complete douchebags about the whole thing. Totally unhelpful."

She huffs an incredulous sigh. "Then we need to talk to them."

I shoot her a sidelong glance, about to tell her how big of a waste of time that'll be, when I stop short. Actually, she's right. Only, it's not *we* who need to talk to the police.

"Sylvie, what if you go?"

"What?"

I clench my jaw. "I don't think they like me."

Understanding washes over her features. "Oh." While we may not be the best of friends, Sylvie knows me. At least the public persona I put forth. Which isn't a very nice one.

"If you talk to them, they might actually listen." There's a reason Sylvie and Brooklyn are friends. Birds of a feather flock together, they say. And Sylvie and Brooklyn are the same exact bird.

She's nodding, liking the idea. "Yeah. Okay."

"Here," I say, "write this down." I open up the emails again and prattle off Brooklyn's case number, as well as any other relevant information I can think of. Within a few minutes, Sylvie is off, and while I'm mostly relieved to have her gone, I'm legitimately hoping that her sweet nature might help our case. She's also the reason we found the footage. I make a silent vow to never be snarky with her ever again.

With Sylvie gone, I let my guard down a bit, allowing myself to sink into Julian's couch cushions. He comes up beside me, having been quiet for most of the last few minutes.

"We can still try to learn everything we can about this guy," Julian suggests, sensing my shift in mood. He leans closer. "Have you gone through all your Instagram DMs like you mentioned before? Maybe there are other clues."

I offer a halfhearted smile. He's only trying to help—to brighten the mood. And even though I'm feeling especially hopeless right now, he's right.

Searching through those messages again can't hurt.

"And I'm sure Sylvie will make progress with the police." He gingerly sits down beside me with an amused smile.

I nod. At least someone is thinking straight. I don't know what's wrong with me. I guess the situation is just starting to feel hopeless. But if I lose momentum now, it could mean the difference between Brooklyn's life or death.

I think back to the footage, not wanting to rewatch it. While the guy's entire head was covered, at least I could make out his height, his build.

Julian leans back against the couch cushions, and I settle next to him, our elbows almost touching, as I bring my knees up underneath me. I'd started a list at work today. A list of guys I suspected could be behind this. I push away the nagging thought of this whole thing being futile and search the first profile.

Hours later, I've eliminated dozens of guys just based on build and height alone, and I think Julian can sense my composure melting. My frustration, my panic. Usually, I'm good at keeping it all together. At not letting anyone see anything beyond a cold smile. But I guess these are extenuating circumstances.

"I have leftovers in the fridge if you want some," Julian says, reaching out to touch my arm. I stare at his fingers grazing along my forearm. I'm about to protest when my stomach grumbles.

"Is it that late already?" I ask.

He shrugs. "I'll get it for us."

"Where's your roommate?" I ask, suddenly

realizing that we've been here for hours without any sighting of him. I can't say I even know what he looks like. We've probably passed each other in the halls at some point, but I never knew who he was.

"Oh, uh, he's out of town," Julian calls over his shoulder from the kitchen. "At least I think so. I don't know, he doesn't tell me much." He chuckles.

"He didn't tell you?" I ask. That seems so weird. Although I guess some roommates are like that.

He shrugs. "We're not that close. Not like you and Brooklyn."

I guess that makes sense. But wouldn't it be polite to tell your roommate you'd be gone? I suppose guys act differently toward each other too. They're a little less paranoid about the other one being kidnapped. Girls, we're always on alert.

And now I know why.

God. I rub my forehead, feeling a headache beginning to build. My back is aching too. It gets worse when I'm stressed. I've been trying to avoid the pain pills. Even though I have a prescription for them, it seems icky to be hooked on them as a college-aged kid. I don't want to depend on them. So, I just suffer instead. Probably why I'm moody all the time.

I hear the microwave ding, and Julian comes back with two plates of something I don't quite recognize. A rice dish of some sort.

"It's kind of the only thing I know how to make," Julian says sheepishly, handing me a plate. "It's Korean. My mom would make it for me and my sister all the time growing up."

I smile thinking about Julian as a little kid. "It looks good," I say. And it really does. Fried rice with beef and veggies.

"Are all those yours?" I ask, inclining my head toward the controllers in the corner.

He cracks a smile. "Oh yeah . . ." He shoots me a guilty look. One I see often. As if video games are the epitome of laziness and unintelligence. I get it. I've given the same response dozens of times. Albeit with more of a "bite me" glare.

I laugh. "No judgment. We already swapped *Sims* stories."

He shrugs. "True. I've been really into this horror game lately. It's some Slenderman knockoff."

"Oh, I love Slenderman."

He laughs. "Right? I scream like a little girl."

I snort. "I can see you screaming like a little girl."

He shoves me in the arm. Lightly. I pretend it rocks me more than it actually does. It's the game. We both know what we're doing. His hand slides down my arm and rests over my fingers. He squeezes them. I shift slightly to lean closer to him, and my back hurts. I wince, but it's practically imperceptible. I know because I've done it hundreds of times.

Julian's hand leaves mine to rest on my shoulder. "Does your back hurt?" he asks, his hand running down my spine.

I frown, looking up at him. Yes. Yes, it does. But nobody knows that. I don't talk about it. Ever. Brooklyn is the only one in this town with any knowledge of that. I don't appear outwardly disabled, and I like it that way.

I'm almost angry. It's not something people get to know about me. "How did . . ." I search for words.

"You just—" he stammers, probably noticing my alarm. "You act like you're in pain sometimes."

No, I do *not*.

As if he can read my mind, he adds, "Not out in public. I never noticed it before. You've just seemed in pain the last few days. In your apartment. Or right now . . ."

I stare at him. No one's ever brought it up to me before. But I suppose I have been letting my guard down with him. Weirdly. And I am in more pain than usual. It's the stress. The bad sleep. Julian keeps rubbing his hand up and down my back. It feels nice. Warm. Comforting. He pulls me against him, and I rest my head on his shoulder.

He's seen more sides of me the last few days than most people have, honestly. I practically had a breakdown in front of him. It's possible that I've forgotten his presence, let my pain show more than usual. It is constant, after all.

"Yeah," I let myself say. "I have chronic back pain. Stress makes it worse sometimes."

His hand stills on my back. "Oh. I'm sorry." And he sounds genuine. Not the fake pity that made me stop telling people in the first place. It's sweet, I guess. That he actually seems to care.

There's a long pause before Julian takes in a breath. He seems to hesitate a moment before blurting, "Since I spent the other night on your couch, do you want to spend tonight on mine?"

I giggle into his shoulder. "Yeah, but let's play one of your horror games first."

Chapter 19

It's been five days since Brooklyn went missing. Five whole days. I try to ignore that statistic we've all heard about how the longer a missing person goes without being found, the less likely there is to be a good outcome. Sure, it's probably true for most cases. But not for this one. Not for Brooklyn.

I force myself to shower, realizing it's been too long since the last one. Julian and I stayed up way too late last night playing some super creepy video game that made both of us scream multiple times. He's right. He does scream like a girl. And it's hilarious.

We woke up snuggled together on his couch this morning. He had some meeting with a professor he had to run off to, so I made my way back home to shower and harass the police about the footage I sent them. I wonder if Sylvie made any headway with them yesterday.

I wait until 9 a.m., giving them more than enough time to check their email, survey the footage, and come to some sort of conclusion. I dial the local police department, and after explaining myself multiple times to multiple people, I'm put through to someone who's familiar with my "case." I hate that word. Like Brooklyn is nothing more than a number.

"Hi, yes, we did receive your email. Thank you," the woman on the end of the line says.

"And?" I question, trying my hardest not to sound pushy.

She sighs. "Unfortunately, the person isn't identifiable. It's helpful in that we know what happened, but it doesn't really give us any leads."

I'm stunned into silence. I mean, I guess I knew the person's face was obscured and his license plate was unreadable. But can't they do something?

"We know now that it was a kidnapping, so her case is being moved to the appropriate department," the officer says as if that should give me some kind of hope.

"And you'll find her," I state.

"We'll do our best."

The conversation fizzles from there. I try to get more out of her, but she doesn't budge. She vaguely mentions Sylvie's presence at the station, but doesn't say anything further. And just like that, I'm back where I started. Sending them the footage did virtually nothing. They don't care. Her case has been moved to a different department, whatever that means.

I grit my teeth, grabbing my phone, my cup of coffee, my keys, and walking to the door. I jog down the stairs, slamming the front door open and stalking across the parking lot. It's nice out today. Sunny, not too hot. A day I'd normally use to take a walk around the neighborhood. Maybe even go on a hike somewhere.

But no. Today, I will be sitting in my car with a cup of coffee, watching the parking lot. I may not have the fucker's license plate, but I do know what his car looks like.

I hop into the driver's seat and slam the door shut. It's not hot enough yet that the car will turn into an oven. Maybe later I'll need to crack a window, but for now I'm fine. I lean back, crisscrossing my legs in the seat beneath me.

I'm parked on the far side of the lot, facing out. It's a perfect vantage point. I can see everything from here. I do a quick scan. The car from the footage was a silver SUV. I don't know the make or model, but I know I could recognize it if I saw it. And I don't see it here.

It doesn't seem too farfetched that he could come back to the scene of the crime. What if he needs something of Brooklyn's? He has her car keys—what if he comes back to take her car? I glance to the corner; it's still there.

And who knows? Maybe this has nothing to do with Sarah's Instagram profile and was just a random kidnapping. Maybe he lives in the building. Or nearby.

So, I settle myself with my phone and coffee at hand—and I wait.

Two hours in, I end up cracking the window. It's starting to get hot. At least I'm in the shady part of the lot. I've seen numerous people come and go by now. Many I recognize. They're mostly college students. A few silver SUVs drive by, temporarily spiking my adrenaline, but none are the car from the video.

As I debate whether or not to go make myself another cup of coffee, a violent rap startles me. I suck in a breath, turning to see a figure standing on the passenger side of my vehicle. My brain registers who it is almost instantly, but my body doesn't catch up. I yelp anyway.

"God. Julian." I roll down the window.

He grins, leaning in, his forearms resting on sill. "What are you doing in here?"

I give him a long look, knowing he'll probably tell me I'm wasting my time. "Just sitting."

He raises his eyebrows. "And how long have you been just sitting?"

I shrug. "A few hours."

His grin fades a bit. "You're watching for the car, aren't you?" When I don't respond, he continues, "What makes you think it would even come back here?"

"I don't know!" I take a deep breath, purposefully lowering my voice back to normal. "I just . . . the police got the footage. And they don't care. So, I'm the only person who's looking for her, who's—"

The passenger door opens, and Julian slides inside. I watch him, the rest of my sentence fizzling on my tongue.

"I'll join you. We'll watch for the car."

I blink. "Thank you," I say softly.

He smiles—one of those cute genuine smiles that I'm beginning to wonder might mean something more. But in a flash, he's all business. "Okay, what's our game plan? How can I be useful?"

I arch an eyebrow. "Actually, you really want to be useful? You could go get me another coffee." I hold up my empty cup, and he chuckles.

***

We spend most of the day sitting in the hot car with the windows rolled down watching the parking lot and talking about stupid shit. About our goals for after college. Our fears. Whether time travel exists. About the beginning of the universe and how it will end. And if it's even worth it for us to find out. We're not going to be there, so why should we care? Julian declares that the pursuit of knowledge is what defines us as human beings and therefore understanding our own demise is critical to our humanity. My opinion is slightly more nihilistic. No surprise there. He finds it entertaining though.

Like with most of our pursuits thus far, Julian eventually persuades me to go back inside. We've watched the parking lot for hours at this point, and I'm beginning to realize the futility in my actions.

"We can look over the footage again," Julian suggests. "Maybe you missed something. I can go through it this time; I haven't even seen it."

I shrug, following him through the front doors and up the stairs. He could be right. I did practically squeeze my eyes shut and rush through the video. Not that anyone could blame me. Watching my best friend get kidnapped is not really something I'd like to relive. And while I'd gone through the footage again earlier today, I'd barely squinted my way through it. Maybe a fresh set of eyes would be good. A more objective pair too.

Julian follows me into my apartment as comfortably as if he lives here. It's odd. We've really only known each other for a handful of days, and he's become the only person I can confide in. Talk to. Be with. At least with Brooklyn gone.

I reach around him to set my keys on the entryway table, my shoulder brushing against his arm. He doesn't move out of the way, and part of me wonders if it's on purpose. Because suddenly I'm standing way, way too close to him, my keys forgotten, his fingers reaching out to touch my wrist. I look up and can't help but remember the moment from yesterday. When our breath was so close, I could hardly breathe.

He gently slides his fingers from my wrist up my arm, then slowly envelops me in a hug. I've never been much of a hugger. Not super touchy feely. But for some reason, this hug is different. I don't mind hugging Julian. I might even like hugging Julian. I press my ear against his chest, his heartbeat hammering against me. And for the first time in five days, I feel . . . calm? Or at least the closest to calm

I'm capable of feeling.

He pulls away just enough so that our foreheads touch, his breath warm against my cheek. My gaze studies the crease of his lips, my brain fuzzy. His arms tighten around me, his fingers drawing idle circles on my shoulder.

The space between us evaporates, slowly—like dew on morning grass—when suddenly he pulls back, his head turning.

"What?" I breathe.

His gaze has slipped past mine and is glued to something over my shoulder. "I—" he stammers. I turn to see what's distracted him. My laptop, open to a still of the footage I'd been reviewing earlier. It shows the figure and the car.

He takes a small step back, his hands sliding down my arms. "Is that the car?" he asks.

I glance between him and the screen. "Yeah. Why?"

He stalks forward, kneeling on the ground in front of the couch, pulling the laptop closer. He presses play and watches. The figure comes into view, dragging Brooklyn with him. Not wanting to see it again, instead, I watch Julian. His expression has contorted into something strange. Confusion, shock, fear, disbelief.

"What is it?" I ask.

Suddenly, through my barely open front door, comes a noise. Julian jerks his head in the direction. "I think that was my apartment door." He stands.

"Your apartment?" I ask distractedly, still caught up on the footage, on my question he hasn't answered. "Maybe your roommate came home." I shrug; it doesn't matter.

"Yeah," he says slowly, swiftly walking to the door, opening it, and peering out into the hallway. I watch him, confused. It's highly unlikely someone would break into one of the apartments here, if that's what he's worried about. And he still hasn't answered my damn question about the car.

"Carter!" he yells, startling me.

And then he's gone.

"Wha—Julian?" I utter, jogging to the doorway to see him disappearing around the corner. I hear him yelling, hear footsteps running down the stairs. What the fuck is he doing? I halfheartedly follow, reaching the stairs and looking down. They're both gone. Where, I don't know. I guess his roommate came back? And left again?

I wait a few seconds more, my heartrate still high after Julian's shout. A couple minutes later, he returns, striding up the staircase as if on a mission.

"What was that?" I demand, but he doesn't answer. And instead of heading back to my apartment, he enters his own.

I follow. "Was it your roommate?"

He hesitates for half a second. Long enough for me to notice. "Yeah. He—he didn't hear me. Then he drove off."

I frown. "He didn't hear you?"

Julian shrugs. "I guess not." But even he doesn't seem to believe the lie.

"You yelled at him."

One, two, three seconds go by. "Yeah. Weird, right?" He laughs but it's not a real laugh. I can tell. Julian is a bad liar. Or at least I think he is. I don't know him that well. It's only now hitting me. Maybe he's a great liar, but this is just too big of a lie.

"That's really weird."

"Yeah," he breathes. He walks away from me, disappearing down the hallway and into one of the rooms. I simply stare after him in silence. Because suddenly, something is off. Way off. Something is *wrong*.

I glance around the apartment. If his roommate did come home, he couldn't have been here long, because nothing has really changed. I enter the kitchen, continuing to glance around. What could've gotten Julian so upset? Maybe he and Carter have more of a contentious relationship than I'd realized.

"Julian, I—"

I'm debating grabbing myself a drink of water—suddenly realizing how thirsty I am—when my eyes snag on something in the corner, on the floor. Something I couldn't have seen from any other angle, something I would have easily overlooked during any of my other times here.

A pair of keys.

My breath hitches in my throat, because I don't need a closer look to know whose they are. But I force my feet forward anyway, making my way around the dining room table to the car keys lying on the floor in the corner, obscured by chairs and the layout of the apartment.

I grab them with shaking fingers. The pink pom-pom, the sticky key fob.

And holding them in my hands makes it all official. Real. Sudden footsteps down the hallway cause the keys to slip from my hands, clattering against the floor, pulling the air from my lungs with it.

Brooklyn's car keys.

Chapter 20

The keys bounce against the linoleum, skidding to a stop at my feet.

"You okay?" Julian calls.

I scramble to pick them up, and hunch myself into the corner, out of sight from the hallway. "Yeah—fine," I choke out. I pull in a shuddering breath, staring down at the keys sparkling in my hands, making sure I'm right. Because how can this be real? How can Julian—Julian Sun, the boy I've been obsessed with since freshman year—have *anything* to do with Brooklyn's disappearance? Anything at all? He's been just as invested as me since day one. He's been *helping* me.

Or maybe not. He kept distracting me from any of my surveillance—not that it was all that effective to start with. He just showed up. For no reason at all. And maybe it wasn't a coincidence. And then he'd seen the footage . . .

I pull out my phone, pulling up Sarah's profile. Surely, I would have remembered if Julian Sun was one of the guys I'd catfished. Of course I would. But I double check anyway. No. No sign of him.

"Vally?" Julian calls. "I think . . . this is going to sound crazy . . ."

But I'm barely listening to him. Brooklyn's keys are damning evidence. Regardless of his motive, he had to be the one who did it.

He kidnapped Brooklyn.

And maybe I'm next.

And I know I should be terrified right now, fearful for my life. That I've let a possible kidnapper into my home, my life, and that we're in the same apartment, and he's ready to do God-knows-what to me.

But instead, I'm just fucking mad.

I reach for the knife set on the kitchen counter, yanking out the largest one. I'm done with this shit. And Julian is going to give me answers. Now.

"Julian," I bark, storming into the living room.

He rounds the corner from the hallway, and in the span of half a second, he takes in my expression, my stance, and then his gaze settles on the knife in my hand. "Whoa, what . . . ?" he says slowly.

I roughly chuck Brooklyn's keys at him, and his arms flail, both to protect himself and to catch it. "Tell me what the fuck that is," I demand.

Utter bewilderment settles over his face before he even glances down at the keys. But when he does, he immediately looks back at me, his expression pleading. "Vally. What are these?"

"They're her fucking keys, Julian!" I shout. "Why do you have Brooklyn's keys?"

He stares down at them, dumbfounded. "I—I

swear, Vally. I don't have anything to do with this." He leans forward, but I cut him off.

"You take one step toward me, and I swear I'll throw this knife at your neck," I yell.

His eyes widen, and he holds his hand out, placating. "It's not what it looks like," he repeats.

"You keep saying that, yet I'm not becoming any more convinced."

He clenches his fists together, swallowing.

"I *trusted* you," I spit, my throat closing up, choking on my words. Because my trust doesn't come easy. It's pulled, disentangled, yanked from me. And even after all that, he's ground it into the dirt.

Just like Matt did.

Tears are clawing their way out of my eyes, but I furiously fight them back. I am not going to cry. I am not going to give him the satisfaction.

Julian must see me falling apart at the seams, because he takes a desperate step forward. "Vally," he pleads.

"Get away from me!" I shriek, wielding the knife. "Where is she?" I demand.

He's shaking his head. "I don't know, I swear I don't know. Please believe me."

But there are her keys, clenched between his fingers. Any evidence I'd ever need. I'm staring him down, my expression devoid of empathy. And to think I *liked* this asshole. That I thought he was a good person, someone I could trust. A pang of hurt so sharp courses through me, but I stamp it down.

I've been good at converting pain to rage for a long, long time.

"I recognized the car in the footage," he says quickly.

I already figured that. "As yours?" I snap, suddenly realizing that I've never seen his car. He never drove anywhere.

"No, no," he stutters. "God. This sounds crazy, but—the car, the figure in the footage, the fact that he's been gone since Brooklyn started missing—I didn't think it was true until . . ." He stares down at the keys. "This."

My eyes are narrowed, taking it in. What is he talking about?

"Vally, I didn't kidnap Brooklyn. But I think my roommate did."

Chapter 21

My mind is running in circles, my brain battling my heart. Julian has to be telling the truth. He has to be. He couldn't have had anything to do with it.

But do I just *want* that to be true?

"Your roommate," I echo.

He nods. "It all makes sense. Especially after seeing the footage. That's his car. I know it's his car."

I'm still gripping the knife between my fingers, my eyes narrowed. Because regardless of how genuine he seems right now, I'm becoming acutely aware of how dangerous my trust could be. What might happen if I'm mistaken. Julian Sun, Julian Sun. The sweet boy from English class.

A liar?

A kidnapper?

Or innocent?

He must see the distrust painted across my face, because suddenly he looks pained. "*God*," he moans, running his hands over his face. "I'm so, so sorry, Vally. I should have known—I should have known. He was always weird, but—"

"How could you let this happen?" The words slip out before I can stop them. Because if Julian is truly innocent, I realize how unfair they are.

But his face simply crumples as if he agrees with me completely. "Like I said, I don't know Carter that well. He's basically just an acquaintance." He shakes his head. "But you're right. He started going on and on about how he was tricked into cheating on his girlfriend and how it blew up his life. That's all I knew. I didn't even know anything about the Sarah account until you told me—and even then, I never connected it to him. I just figured he was ranting." Shocked realization is setting over him, mixing with guilt, hunching him over, crumpling in on himself.

"Where are they?" I ask, my voice low, the question aimed practically at the universe—anything that can give me an answer.

"That's the thing," Julian says slowly. "He wore a mask in the footage, and I can't imagine he'd . . ." He swallows. "He can't be a killer—he can't. He must have just wanted to scare her. But—but it's been so long."

My fingers are gripping the knife so tightly, they're starting to hurt.

He holds up his hands helplessly. "Something must have gone wrong."

And this is when the fear hits me. Real, deep fear. Almost more than when I'd initially figured out she was missing, when I found her abandoned groceries in the car. Because if the kidnapping plan went awry, then Brooklyn isn't safe at all. If she's even . . .

"I swear I knew nothing, Vally. Please believe me. I truly wanted to help you find Brooklyn."

My eyes are glazing over, practically shutting him out. Because regardless of whether Julian knew about it or not, how *did* this go so wrong? Was what we did so terrible? Helping girls finally let go of their cheating boyfriends? Catching them in the act? My jaw clenches. Guys say we're crazy when they're the ones who gaslight us, harass us, threaten us. Kidnap us. Kill us.

And break our fucking hearts over and over again.

No, they're the crazy ones.

And Carter might just have met his match.

"Do you believe me?" he asks, his voice wavering.

"I don't know, Julian," I say slowly, coming to the inevitable realization. That however badly I want to believe in him, I can't afford to. Not yet.

Chapter 22

I've decided to continue to let Julian help me, regardless of my suspicions. To his credit, he does seem pretty cut up about the whole thing.

But boo-fucking-hoo. I'll figure out his feelings later. My feelings, too, for that matter. All that matters now is finding Brooklyn.

I'm sitting on the floor six feet away from him, the kitchen knife lying beside my thigh. I'm not quite ready to put it away yet. Because regardless of how much my heart wants to leap into his arms and believe him, if I'm wrong, it could mean death for both Brooklyn and me. And I just can't risk it.

And secondly, I'm just pissed off. And I like how his eyes keep flicking to the knife every once in a while, wondering if I'll pick it up. Wondering if I'll finally let my rage overtake me and fling it at his head.

But no, I'll save that for Carter—the one I *know* is guilty.

His name sounds familiar, but it's not like I remember all the guys I've chatted up under her guise. I open Sarah's account and check the messages, typing his name into the search bar.

And there he is. Carter. From eight months ago. And I don't even have to stalk the profile, check the messages, to know it's him. It has to be.

"So, you're sure the car in the footage is his?" I say.

He nods.

"And you haven't seen the car since?"

"Not since earlier today when I chased him out of the building. He drove off. I swear, I would've tackled him to the ground for answers if I'd reached him."

I'm suddenly so angry that I didn't know the truth just mere hours ago. That Brooklyn's kidnapper was out in our hallway just walking free. I may be shorter and smaller than Julian, but no way in hell would I have let Carter get away from this building unscathed.

"At least now we know *he's* okay," Julian adds.

I level him with an incredulous look. "What a goddamn relief."

"No—all I mean is that we saw him. We know he's . . . alive? Still in town?"

It's true, I guess. We know he's still around. Doing what, though? I'm sick to my stomach at the possibilities. Either Brooklyn is caged up somewhere, or she's—

I cut it off there, unable to entertain the unthinkable.

"So why would he hold on to her for so long? Why hasn't he, I don't know, demanded a ransom? Or whatever the hell kidnappers do?" I ask.

Julian frowns. "I don't know. The only thing I can think is . . ."

"What?" I snap.

He shrugs. "He had on that ski mask—the one we saw in the video. The only thing I can think of happening is that somehow Brooklyn actually saw him. His face. She figured out who he was."

I'm silent for a heartbeat as things click into place. "And now he can't just let her go," I finish for him.

He nods. "Exactly. At least, that's one of the more hopeful outcomes."

He's right, but I bristle at his mention of it. "So, what do we do?"

Julian is silent, working his jaw, staring down at the carpet between us. "I don't know where he would have gone. His car turned right out of the parking lot, toward Larch Street, but he could have gone anywhere after that. It doesn't help. And he doesn't have family in town. And I don't know any of his close friends, so I have no idea if they're in on it too." He looks up at me now, eyes rimmed with desperation. He knows I still suspect him. That he doesn't have my full trust. Not like he did. It's crazy to think he ever had it at all. The last man I trusted was Matt, and I promised to never end up in the same position again. And look where it got me.

For a moment, I empathize with Julian. While I was initially scared of him, unsure what he might do and if he was somehow part of Carter's scheme, I've settled on the realization that Julian is most likely no threat. He means what he says. I think.

He looks down at his lap, to his hands, fiddling aimlessly with a frayed edge on his jeans. "Why . . ." But he stops short, the rest of his sentence fizzling into the stiff air around us.

My head snaps up. "Why what?" I prompt.

He sucks in a breath through his teeth, obviously regretting his one simple word. "Why did you guys start the account?" When my brows knit closer together, he rushes on. "I don't mean it in an accusatory way. Nothing excuses Carter for what he's done. I just . . ."

My eyes narrowed, I wait for him to continue. Because I've heard this question countless times. Why? Why would you do this?

He meets my gaze. "You implied the other night that you're not a good person. I didn't know what you meant—then you told me about the account, and I knew that's what you were talking about. But you're wrong." He shrugs. "You might be quiet, and you might not like many people, but you're not a bad person. Based on how hard you've tried to find Brooklyn, I'd say you're *good*. You're certainly better than me."

I wait, unsure if he's done. The silence stretches long enough that Julian starts to look nervous, and for a brief moment, I relish it. But more importantly, I'm not sure what I'm willing to tell him. An hour ago, I might have spilled my heart out on this god-awful shag carpet. But now?

I sigh, then click my jaw. "I've only ever been in love once," I tell him. His eyes widen just a bit—at the fact that I've been in love or the fact that I'm telling him, I'm not sure. "He was my entire world for two years. And he did everything right. He told me how pretty I was, how much he loved me. He bought me gifts on Valentine's Day. We met each other's families and spent all our time together. Except he wasn't doing everything *right*. He was just doing the right things to get what he wanted. Which was to fuck me."

Julian winces ever so slightly. Funny how the age-old story is just as shocking every time it's told.

"And in the meantime, he was chatting with whatever girls he could find. At school, dating apps, Instagram—wherever." I level him with stare, daring him to argue. "No one deserves to be strung along like that. That's why I started the account."

His wince has deepened into a grimace—something multilayered and profoundly sad. At first, I think it's rooted in pity and am about to shoot some scathing remark his way, but I stop myself. Because it's not quite pity I see in his eyes, but understanding. An inherent understanding that can only come from experience.

But now is not the time to air our dirty laundry.

I rub my forehead where a headache is beginning to grow. "Okay. Carter. What about . . ." I stare at the ceiling, thinking, and Julian immediately straightens, his attention back to the task at hand.

"Places he frequents, favorite coffee shops—we can go by and ask if they've seen him. Where does he work? We can talk to his coworkers. Or, like, any hiking trails he goes to a lot? Places he'd camp out?"

"Actually," Julian starts.

I raise my eyebrows. "Camping sites?" I prompt. "It's super conceivable. It's warm enough now that they could be somewhere remote."

He shakes his head. "No." He abruptly stands and strides across the room.

I scramble up off the floor.

Julian starts rifling through a small table by the couch. "Work. I'm looking for his work keys."

I bite the inside of my lip, trying to follow his train of thought. Before I can ask him to clarify, he stops what he's doing and spins toward me. "He works for the school. In the biology department. But since school's out, he's not actually working this summer. The buildings are empty. But he has keys."

My eyes widen. "You think he's camping out in the science building."

"It's a possibility." With that, he goes back to what he was doing, turning over piles of clutter and junk mail.

I glance around the apartment. "Where does he normally keep them? Wouldn't they just be attached to his car keys?"

Julian shakes his head. "They're not. And he doesn't have a specific place for them. I've seen them just lying around."

"What do they look like?" I begin feebly wandering around.

"It's a keycard, like our student ID cards, with a green lanyard." Julian finishes up at the table and then hurries down the hall. He beelines to one of the rooms, the same one he'd disappeared in earlier after he'd chased after Carter. Only now do I realize that it must be Carter's room. That he'd gone there in search of . . . what? Evidence? My brain bends to my heart just an inch more. Julian is just Julian. An innocent man.

I follow to see him rummaging through his desk and then his bedside table, flipping things over. He returns to the main room, but eventually stops, turning to me. "I don't think they're here."

"Is there a plausible reason he'd have them?" I ask.

He grimaces. "Not really; he's not working during the summer."

"Would they have taken his keys away?" I suggest.

He shakes his head in a firm no. "I have mine for my department. We'll both be working next year so they let us keep the badges."

We stare at each other, both settling on the same firm conclusion. He's at the school. He has to be. The empty, locked science building. The perfect place to hide out. And that means Brooklyn is there too.

Chapter 23

Ten minutes later, we've gathered our things, piled into my SUV, and are heading toward the university, "Kokomo" blasting on my speakers.

"Can you turn it down?" Julian suggests.

"That is unfortunately no longer a feature this car possesses."

"I'm assuming turning it off completely is also not a feature?"

"Bingo." But college students are supposed to have crappy cars, right? At least mine runs. If only on Beach Boys magic.

I pull into campus, driving slowly. We pass the residence halls, coming up on the department buildings. Julian sucks in a breath the moment I turn into the science building parking lot. I see it too. Carter's car. The one from the video.

And suddenly this all feels way too real. Because he's here. This is where he is. This is the car that kidnapped Brooklyn, and it's here. *She's* here. My hands are practically shaking as I pull into the parking lot, away from Carter's car and hopefully not too noticeable. I cut the engine, "Kokomo" coming to an abrupt end.

We both sit in silence for a moment, our gazes fixed on the tall building in front of us.

"What now?" Julian asks.

It's the same question running through my head, so I don't answer for a moment. "Well," I eventually utter. "We can't get in ourselves. They lock the buildings once school is out of session. So, unless we have a key to this specific building . . ."

Julian nods along. "So, either we break in somehow or we wait for Carter?"

Breaking in seems unreasonable. It's a newer building—no rattling doors or rusty windows. And I'm guessing it has a pretty good alarm system. So that's moved to the back burner for now. And waiting for Carter at this point just feels infuriatingly slow. I've been making myself crazy for days over Brooklyn's disappearance and now, here we are—ninety-nine percent sure of Brooklyn's whereabouts—and we have to just wait. Again.

I huff loudly, leaning back against the seat. My back is practically screaming at me after spending two nights in a row on a couch. But it's only fueling my anger. I'm going to tear Carter limb from limb when I see him. He'll be in way more pain than I'm in.

Julian attempts feeble conversation every once in a while, to which I immediately shut him down. After a few more tries, he gives up, and we simply watch the front doors in silence. We're close enough to see through the windows and into the lobby hallway. Close enough to know if anyone is inside—at least near the door. Hours go by without any sight of human activity. Which is normal for summer.

But Carter has to be in there. His car is a dead giveaway.

It's when night begins to fall that I'm startled back to alertness by Julian's hand on my arm.

"Look," he hisses.

My head snaps up, eyes zeroing in on the building. Lights. From what I recall, most of the newer buildings on campus have motion sensor lights. And the lobby is currently illuminated. Seconds later, the door swings open.

And there stands Carter.

Or, at least, what I assume is Carter. I shoot Julian a questioning look, and he vigorously nods. I reach for the door handle, but Julian stops me.

"Wait! We can't scare him off now. We need to find Brooklyn first."

As with many other instances, he's right. Which makes me angry, but the end goal is what matters here, so I refrain from the urge to sprint across the parking lot and tackle Carter to the ground.

We lower ourselves in the car, hoping he isn't suspicious of its presence. There are still security officers, cleaning crew, and grounds people on campus during the summer months.

But he doesn't even glance our way. He strides to his car, gets in, and drives off.

As soon as he's rounded the corner, I glance back at the door. It's open, standing still. But I know it won't last for long. It's one of those timer doors—the ones that stay open for ten seconds then slowly, slowly close.

I throw my car door open and bolt across the lot.

"Vally!" Julian calls, but I ignore him.

I see the door hinge click; it's beginning to close. My sneakers smack across the pavement, and I dart through the garden out front, ignoring the pathway. I practically trip myself to make it in time, jamming my arm between the door and the latch, gaining entrance by just a few seconds.

Julian is not far behind me, and we slip quietly into the building.

The light is still on, and the building is eerily quiet. Not the bustle of footsteps and echo of voices you become accustomed to hearing in university halls. The rooms and hallways beyond the lobby are dark, waiting for a reason for the light sensors to turn on.

Julian takes in a breath, about to speak, just as I cup my hands around my mouth and shout, "Brooklyn!" It echoes down the dark hallways.

He smacks me in the arm. "What are you doing?" he hisses.

I shoot him an incredulous look. "Carter isn't here. We saw him drive off."

Realization settles over his features, but I don't wait for him to agree. I start off down the main hallway, the lights clicking to life as I go.

"Brooklyn!" I call again, beginning to run. Julian calls out her name as well. I don't bother looking in dark rooms—if she was in one, her motion would alert the light sensors. The hallway eventually loops around, back to the lobby. To my right is a large, metal staircase. There are four stories in the building, and from here I can see every one, right on top of each other, balconies overlooking the lobby below.

Julian catches up to me right as I begin my way to the second floor. "You take the right side, I'll take the left," I order as we reach the second floor. He nods, turning sharply and jogging into the darkness.

I scan the classrooms as I make my way down my assigned hallway. They're all dark. Every one of them. I slip into a hall littered with professors' offices, but those are dark too.

A sudden thought halts my perusal. Should we be checking every room? If Brooklyn is unconscious, she wouldn't be triggering the lights.

But Carter was most likely with her only moments before. How long do the lights stay on?

I trot to the balcony, looking down into the lobby. Florescent bulbs still illuminate the area, but it's only been minutes since we came up the stairs. I'm about to turn back and continue down the hallway when a noise freezes me to the spot.

At first, I think it's Julian, but when I hear the front door clang against its hinges, I know it's not. Footsteps cross the lobby floor, and before I can be seen, I shuffle backward, away from the balcony railing.

In the silence, Carter's first step on the metal staircase might as well be a gunshot. I twirl, padding as quietly as I can back into the narrow hallway of professors' offices. Unless one of these rooms is where he's headed, he won't see me when he passes by.

Carter's shoes clack against the stairs and echo in the quiet building. I lean against the wall farthest back, my breathing shallow, eyes closed tight, listening. His footsteps are steady, even paced. Until suddenly, they stop.

And all I can hear is my breathing.

At first, I worry that maybe he's spotted Julian. That he didn't know Carter had returned and accidentally walked into his line of sight.

But then it hits me. Probably only a few seconds after it hit Carter.

The lights.

My hand flies to my mouth. The lights are all on, and Carter has been gone.

Suddenly his footsteps resume, faster this time—he's running up the staircase. But he doesn't stop on the second floor like I expect him to. He keeps going. I can hear him. The clanging metal ends, but soft, quick footsteps patter down a linoleum hallway.

I swallow, slowly emerging from my hideout. A moment later, I see Julian peering around a corner across the way. Our eyes meet, and I know he's come to the same conclusion that I have. I can see the fear in his eyes from twenty feet away.

Carter knows we're here.

Chapter 24

Julian scurries around the balcony to my side, and we retreat to the relative safety of the professors' offices. Not since Carter's retreating footsteps have we heard any noise above us.

"He knows someone's in the building," Julian whispers.

I nod. "The lights."

"The lights," he repeats.

I bite my lip, thinking. "What floor did he go to?" I eventually ask.

"I think third?" Julian guesses. "That's just based on how long I could hear his footsteps on the stairs."

Third was my guess too. What's even on the third floor? More classrooms, I suppose. I rub my temples, squinting my eyes shut. We need a new plan now. There's no hope of finding Brooklyn alone and escaping without a confrontation. Carter is most definitely with her now. Possibly even trying to flee.

That thought wakes me up a bit. I turn to Julian. "How bad could a confrontation really get?" I ask him. "It's two against one. What can he do?"

Julian nods along with me, but his eyes tell a different story. A story I already know but am trying to ignore. Yes, a confrontation could go batshit crazy. Of course it could. But what's the alternative?

Calling the police, I suppose.

But I have this awful feeling nagging at me that if we leave now and wait for police protection—if they even give a fuck enough to come—that Carter will have taken Brooklyn and fled by then. This is our only chance.

"Third floor," I say, waiting for Julian's agreement. After a second of hesitation, he nods.

The hallways are all way too bright. Too bright for what we're doing. As we step back into the main area of the second floor, I'm paranoid that somehow Carter can see us. He knows we're coming. Julian starts toward the main stairs when I catch his arm.

"Too loud," I whisper, shaking my head. "We should take the stairwell."

We make our way to the far corner of the second story where the emergency stairwell lies. I pull open the heavy door, wincing as it groans. The moment we step inside, the lights flicker on with an audible pop. I stare upward, into the spiral.

She's up there. And all I have to do is go get her. And after today, this all ends. All of it. The profile, the catfishing, everything. But if Carter somehow doesn't go to jail for what he's done, I will make his life a living hell until the day he dies.

I take the stairs two at a time, Julian right beside me. When we reach the third floor, we stop for a moment to catch our breath, no way of knowing what's on the other side of the heavy industrial door.

Julian pulls it open—slowly, trying to avoid any noise. We step into a dark hallway that flickers to life once our presence is made known. I crinkle my nose and hold in a curse. But beyond our hallway, the lights are on—meaning this is where Carter went. He had to have come by within the last five minutes.

There's no point in delaying the inevitable, so I march forward, scanning the rooms on either side of us for light. So far, nothing. Julian joins me as we make a silent lap around the whole floor, seeing through the windows into dark, empty classrooms. Once we make it back to the stairwell, we give each other quizzical looks.

All the classrooms are dark. There's no way Carter could be in any of them. I open my mouth in confusion, looking around. There's got to be something we've missed. Unless he went on to the fourth floor.

I turn back to Julian to see a grimace on his face. A knowing grimace, like he's just realized some terrible truth. My adrenaline spikes.

He meets my gaze. "The med lab," he whispers in resignation.

I frown. "What?"

"The medical lab."

It takes a moment for that to sink in. The medical lab. For pre-med students. Laboratory stuff. Okay.

"We passed it earlier, but it has no windows. Because of . . . well, you know."

I don't know. What? The pre-med students don't have windows in their classrooms because they're vampires? They'll burn up in the sun? They do top secret shit? "I don't understand."

"Cadavers."

I cluck my tongue, my expression dropping into a glare. "Are you fucking serious?"

"You didn't know there were cadavers on campus?"

"No, Julian, I don't spend much time calculating my proximity to corpses, thank you."

"Well, there are. And they're in there." He tilts his head in the direction of the med lab. We can see the door from where we're standing. And Julian is right. The room has no windows.

I glare harder at Julian, aware that I'm taking out my fear and anger on him. "So, what you're telling me is that we don't know for sure if Carter is in there, but we do know that at least there are a bunch of dead people."

Julian winces.

"I love that."

"It's not like they're just lying out on tables—they have drawers," he reasons.

Great. Dead people drawers. "God, stop talking about them." I turn toward the room. It's about thirty feet away. It's a fair bet that he's in there. It's honestly the best place to hide. No one can see in. No one would know you were there. The more I mull it over, the more I realize it has to be where they are. Where Brooklyn is.

Julian and I lock eyes. I'm not really sure what the plan is here. I can tell he doesn't know either. But what can Carter do? Like we said earlier, it's two against one. And he's just a normal college kid. A young, normal kid. He wouldn't do anything . . . violent.

We pad softly down the hall toward the heavy, windowless door. The door which Carter—and Brooklyn—is on the other side of. I reach for the handle and slowly turn.

Chapter 25

The door is heavy and groans as we push it open. I take in the room as we slowly step inside. Rows of tables, stool chairs stacked in the corner. And the lights are already on. Blazing.

And in a split second, my gaze settles on what really matters.

Brooklyn. She's alive. Relief floods through me because, oh my God, Brooklyn is alive. She's alive and breathing and staring right at me from across the room.

But that relief is quickly replaced by dread when I realize what's happening. Because Carter is there too. Standing, holding her from behind, his arm wrapped around her waist and something sharp pressed to her neck. A scalpel. Waiting for us.

Julian and I halt, the door swinging closed behind us with a thunk.

"Carter," I say slowly, because ultimately, deep down, I can't believe that he'd hurt her. He wouldn't. Normal people don't do terrible things like this. This situation can be salvaged. He won't hurt her. He'll choose the right thing.

But my voice only seems to aggravate him. His muscles tense, the scalpel pressing closer to her neck. "What the hell are you doing here?" he demands, his gaze starting on me and then sliding to Julian.

"I—I couldn't stop her," Julian starts, taking a step forward.

Carter's eyes narrow, and so do mine. He couldn't *what*?

"I figured out it was you," he says. "She got on your tail, and I tried to stop her—I couldn't let her ruin your life. But she figured it out."

Carter's expression remains suspicious. "You figured it out," he says slowly.

"You left her keys in the apartment. I saw your car in her dashcam footage." At Carter's sudden horrified expression, Julian interjects, "Don't worry, there's no license plate. The police can't track you."

"I thought—" Carter stutters, then seems to fall apart. "Things got out of hand, man," he admits. He glances helplessly at Brooklyn. She stands still, her eyes locked on mine, rimmed with the kind of fear I've never seen before.

Julian shakes his head. "I'm here to help you. I've been helping you this whole time. Why do you think I didn't let her come here alone?"

My gaze snaps toward him, settling on his expression. He looks genuine, eyes locked with Carter. He doesn't turn to look at me. And while every part of me wants to believe that this isn't true, that, no, Julian isn't that good of a liar. That all those days spent together, buying me dinner, sleeping on my couch, calming me down, telling me he knew nothing of Brooklyn's kidnapping, could not have just been a lie. They couldn't have been. He wouldn't have done that.

But when he gives me a momentary sidelong glance, I don't know what I see in his eyes. Is it remorse? Compassion? Which is the lie? Right now, or the last five days?

And I realize now, this moment, is not the time to gamble. Not on a man I barely know.

With one last look at Brooklyn—hoping she understands that I'm not abandoning her, that no, it's the opposite—I turn and run for the door.

Carter yells, and Julian turns, but I've already yanked the door open and am out in the hallway. Because this is Brooklyn's last chance. Our last chance. If I can get out of here, I can get help. The police can't ignore me now. They *won't*. I'll drag them here kicking and screaming if I have to.

I just have to get out of here alive. I sprint down the hallway, hearing the med lab door groaning open behind me.

"Vally!" Julian shouts. Footsteps start after me, and another pair runs off in a different direction.

I race for the main stairs, sprinting down, the metal clanging as I go. I can feel Julian gaining on me, and as I near the bottom floor, I see Carter sprint into view, blocking the front doors. He must have taken the stairwell. I reach the floor, taking a sharp left, both men following me.

But with every light flickering to life the second I run by, there's no fucking way to hide. There's a literal beacon lighting my path, telling them where I've gone. I veer left down an already-lit narrow hallway—hopefully before they've rounded the last corner and seen me. Rows of offices line the walls, and I see one with curtains over the window. Praying it's unlocked, I grab for the handle, pushing the door open.

The lights flicker to life, but I quickly shut the door, as quietly as possible. Sinking into a sitting position, my back against the door, I wait, my heart thundering in my chest. I can hear footsteps down the main hallway.

"Where did she go?" Carter shouts.

"I don't know, she—"

"She couldn't have gotten outside."

The footsteps scurry off, in what direction I'm not sure—all I know is that they're leaving, searching for me elsewhere. I breathe a quiet sigh of relief, my hands covering my mouth. It's only then that I realize they're shaking.

A range of emotions course through me. I'm still giddy with relief that Brooklyn is alive. She's alive and breathing, and I saw her with my own two eyes. Because even though I've spent the last five days with the ultimate goal of bringing her home safe and sound, deep inside, I doubted whether there was any part of Brooklyn to bring home safely.

But all that doubt is gone now.

And the terror coursing through my veins—of Carter, now of Julian—is slowly being replaced by resolve. Because now I *know* Brooklyn is okay. Meaning I'll do anything it takes to get her out of here alive.

I haven't heard footsteps for a few minutes, so I'm assuming neither Carter nor Julian are nearby. Surely, I'd hear them. Maybe they're on the opposite end of the building. Maybe they thought I went upstairs. I stand slowly, parting the curtain on the window to look out into the hall. Not that there's much to see. I can barely see five feet in either direction.

I take in a shuddering breath, grasp the handle, and twist. I open the door slowly, silently. As I step out into the hallway, the fluorescent lights set my nerves on fire. I pull the door shut softly behind me, and then I'm off.

I know there's an exit on the other side of the building—opposite the lobby. If I can just make it outside, I can get to my car and drive to the police station. Or, at the very least, dial 911 without the fear of being overheard. I reach one of the main hallways and peer out, both ways, checking for activity. I don't hear or see anyone, so I continue to the left, faster this time.

Either they're genuinely not around, or they're waiting for me. The terrifying thought just spurs me along faster. I can see the glass double doors coming into view. I can make it. I know I can.

Until a figure steps out of an alcove I didn't see, blocking my path. He doesn't move toward me, just simply stands in my way. We lock eyes, and I search his in the silence—for an answer. Why.

"Julian," I say, my voice low, quiet. It's both a plea and a threat.

Something flickers across his expression, but he's too far away for me to tell what exactly it is. I calculate my chances of getting past him. He's bigger than me, sure, but he's not all that strong. His stature is just made up of gangly limbs. But I'm still at a disadvantage—short, small. He wouldn't actually hurt me though . . . would he?

My instinct screams no, but after today—after the last five days of hell—I realize I've been wrong about almost everything. Sarah's profile could never hurt us. No one would ever kidnap Brooklyn. And Julian could never be capable of betraying me. Yet here we are.

I take a step forward, just to see what he'll do. He looks nervous all of a sudden.

"Vally, I'm not—" he starts, barely above a whisper. He glances down the hallway.

But just then, the elevator near us dings, the door sliding back to reveal Carter. Half a sentence is already out of his mouth before his gaze settles on me, the words drying up. He steps off the elevator as I take a frantic step backward. Carter holds up his hands.

"Whoa," he says. "Just wait. We can talk. We can work this out."

I've never heard a lie more apparent. I can see right through to the panic buried underneath. All he cares about is getting out of this free. And Brooklyn and I are just in the way.

But there's not anywhere I can run. Julian is blocking the door, and Carter is slowly making his way out into the hallway. All that's behind me is a classroom. A classroom with no way out. The windows in these buildings don't open more than few inches for circulation. They're not an escape route—even if I could get to one in time.

It's then that Carter runs toward me, Julian right behind him. Instinct backs me into the wall, even though I know there's no way out of this. What can I do? It's Julian who reaches me first, his hand wrapping around my arm. And before I even realize what I'm doing, I've punched him in the face—square in the nose.

He cries out and recoils, letting go of me. I sprint forward, between the two of them, but Carter grasps the hem of my shirt, yanking me back. I elbow him in the stomach, but instead of backing off, he throws himself at me, pushing me to the ground. I struggle, kicking, trying to hurt any part of him I can, but before I know it, he's kneeling against my back, my arms pinned behind me. I hiss through my teeth, refusing to cry out from the pain.

"If you try to run again, I'll kill her," he spits, and that's when I stop struggling. He means it. I know he does. And even if he doesn't, I can't call his bluff now. He notices my calm and leans in closer. "You understand? You won't try to run again?"

I nod.

I'm wincing as the pain in my back intensifies, when all of a sudden, it lets up. Carter stumbles, and I realize it's Julian who's pulled him away. "You don't need to hurt her," he says softly, but there's an edge to his voice. He looks angry, but in a split second, it's gone.

Carter rolls his eyes and yanks me to a standing position. He pulls me down the hallway, into the elevator. Julian steps in after us, standing on my other side. It's only then that I notice the blood running down his face. He holds a hand over his nose, tilting his head up a bit. Good.

"Your phone?" Carter demands, holding out his hand. I reluctantly pull it from my pocket, handing it over. "You know, if you didn't mess with people's lives, you wouldn't be in this situation," he goads. "I had a good thing going with my girlfriend until 'Sarah' ruined it." He snorts.

"Well, maybe if you weren't a cheater, *Sarah* never would have gotten involved. Did you ever think of that?"

He shoots me a glare so hostile I think he might hit me, but just then, the elevator dings. Carter pushes me out into the hallway and then back toward the med lab.

When we enter, I don't see Brooklyn. Could she have gotten away while they were both occupied with me? The hopeful thought is quickly diminished. No, she couldn't have. They wouldn't have left her alone. But she's not here.

"Where's—" I begin before Carter shoves me forward again, cutting me off.

"Open the door," Carter demands, and it's then that I see there's a room within the med lab. With a chair propped up under the handle.

Julian promptly removes the chair and opens the door. It must be a closet or something. Or another, small classroom? I'm not sure what it is until Carter pushes me closer and a waft of cool air overtakes me.

"Wait," I protest halfheartedly, knowing full well it won't do anything.

Carter's grip on my arms tightens, and before I can continue my plea, he's shoved me forward, into the closet, slamming the door behind me. A lone light flickers above. It's cold in here. Too cold. Why is it so cold? Brooklyn is huddled in the middle of the room. Not in a corner, not against the walls . . . because the walls are . . .

I slam a hand over my mouth.

Drawers.

"Fuck you, Julian," I murmur.

Chapter 26

Drawers. With . . . people inside. Dead people. At least, I'm assuming. It's not like I'm going to pull one out and investigate. But what else is this room? This room sitting at thirty-seven degrees, filled with body-sized drawers, sitting in a medical lab used for pre-med students.

My skin crawling, I force my attention to the only thing that matters.

"Brooklyn," I breathe, sinking to my knees in front of her, my hands on either side of her shoulders. "Oh my God." I hug her, and she clings to me.

"What are you doing here? How did you find me?" she asks when we pull away. Her hair is a mess, and there are still faint mascara smudges down her cheeks. She's wearing the same outfit I saw her in on Sunday—the day she disappeared.

I open my mouth, ready to spill the whole story, but I realize it truly just boils down to one thing. "Julian," is all I can say. Because it's true. He brought me here. He *lured* me here.

She nods, tears welling in her eyes. "It's because of Sarah. The profile. Carter's one of the guys."

I nod. "I know. I'm so sorry, Brooklyn. I'm so—so sorry." My voice cracks, despair welling up inside me, crawling its way out. Somehow, I've managed to keep from breaking down this whole time. Brooklyn needed me. Needed me to be strong. But now, here, facing what I've done, I'm unable to stop it.

"No," Brooklyn snaps, grabbing my arm. It's the sternest I've ever seen her, and her grip is sharp enough to stop my tears from falling. "It's not your fault. None of this is your fault."

I shake my head, almost imperceptibly. "If I hadn't come up with the idea, if I hadn't messaged all those guys—"

"Those *men* were caught cheating. You helped those women find closure. That's the end of it. What Carter has done has nothing to do with that. He's a coward who is blaming us for how shitty *he is*." Brooklyn spits the words out like they taste bad on her tongue. I've never seen her so angry. So upset. I suppose five days locked in a medical lab filled with dead bodies would do that to you.

And it's funny. Because I'm normally the one building Brooklyn up. Telling her to stop bending over backward for people, to stand up for herself, to stop doubting herself, to stop blaming herself for the shit other people throw at her. I'm the careless the one, the tough one, the bitch. And here Brooklyn is—in the, arguably, most stressing situation of our lives—holding me together.

"We're going to get out of here," I say. Brooklyn nods slowly. "What happened, anyway?"

Brooklyn suddenly looks tired. So tired. She shakes her head. "He kidnapped me in the parking lot. I'd just gotten home with groceries. He—I was unconscious and woke up here. He went on and on about how luring men into cheating was terrible and how we'd ruined his life. He knew we were both behind it. He knew about you."

I frown. So he knew Brooklyn's photos were only a cover? He knew it was me behind the messages? Why wouldn't he have just kidnapped *me* then? Better than dragging Brooklyn into this. And I'd have given him a much better fight.

"Why'd he go after you?" I think aloud. "If he knew it wasn't you he was talking with, why bother kidnapping someone who wasn't even responsible?" I'm even angrier now. Before, at least Brooklyn was the logical target, even if it was all a disguise. But to purposefully go after the girl in the pictures, knowing she wasn't the one raising all the hell? What a douchebag.

Brooklyn shakes her head. "I don't know. He mentioned something about you being his initial target . . . but—he called you disabled."

My head snaps toward her at the mention. "Disabled?" I repeat. I hate the word. Hate when doctors have used it, when my parents have used it, especially when people who don't fucking know me use it. Because to them, it's almost like a slur. Some sad, pathetic term that they get to glue to my back and shower pity upon. They don't truly know what it means—all they know is a stereotype.

Brooklyn's expression darkens, and she nods sadly. "Said he didn't want to risk actually hurting someone."

I snort. Look where that got him. "He must have somehow looked us up in school records. Or maybe just did some really good internet stalking." It's information that can't be that hard to find. I wonder what else he knows about us. How long he spent researching us, planning, waiting.

"So what's his plan?" I ask.

"Well," Brooklyn starts, "when I woke up, I struggled with him, and I guess he wasn't expecting that. I managed to wrench off his mask, and I saw his face. Then . . . then he wouldn't let me go. Said he didn't know what to do."

I purse my lips. It's not far off from what Julian and I had assumed. Although—what the hell am I talking about? Julian knew the whole time. Julian fucked me over. Tricked me. I glance back at the door. At least, I think he did. Julian, who's a terrible liar. I just can't figure out which is the lie.

But either way, I'm angry. And that anger is mixing with the hurt I'm trying so hard to ignore—creating a horrible Molotov cocktail ready to explode at any minute.

I turn, making my way back to the door. I jiggle the doorknob, but it obviously does nothing. "Hey!" I yell, banging against the metal. It rattles, echoing throughout the small room. "Hey!" I scream, continuing to bang against the door. "Let us out of here, your motherfuckers!"

It takes a few more minutes of me banging on the metal and screaming obscenities before I hear the chair scraping against the floor outside. I take a quick step back. The door opens, and there stands Carter, Julian a few feet behind him.

"Look," Carter starts, leaning against the doorframe as if casually chatting with two friends and not two women he's kidnapped. "This whole thing is not what it looks like."

My eyebrows raise, and I hold in a snort. "Oh really, Carter? I don't know, what does it look like?" I ask. "It looks to me like you kidnapped my best friend because you're butthurt that you got caught cheating on your girlfriend. Is that not the case?"

His eyes narrow, and he straightens just a bit. "Believe what you want, but this was never supposed to get this serious."

"Yeah, kidnapping is never very serious," I snap.

He rolls his eyes, his air of nonchalance settling back over him. "It was just supposed to be, like . . . a prank."

I narrow my eyes, tilting my head.

A prank?

What the actual fuck?

Julian must see the shift in my expression—from anger to a pure, soft rage—because he glances worriedly to Carter.

"It was just supposed to scare you guys," Carter admits. "To stop you from doing this to other men."

I can't help but bark out a laugh. Other men. As if *other men* are the victims. Funny how I set out to prevent girls from experiencing the same hurt and humiliation I did—and in doing so, cheating men became the poor, innocent casualties.

I wish I still had Julian's kitchen knife, because everything in me wants to stab Carter right in the eyes. "First of all, these assholes do this to themselves. It's their girlfriends who reach out and ask me to do it. And second of all, *kidnapping someone is not how you solve problems.*" I'm shouting by the end of my sentence.

But Carter hardly seems phased. Honestly, from everything I've seen from him thus far, I'm beginning to wonder if he's truly psychopathic. We stand there, gazed locked, for what feels like eternity. Carter works his jaw, his expression becoming harder every second. Suddenly Julian's hand grasps his shoulder, momentarily commanding his attention. Carter gives me one last glance before shutting the door and locking us inside with the chair.

I hear low voices, so I approach the door, leaning my ear against it.

"We need to calm down and let them go." It's Julian's voice, that I'm sure of. He sounds calm, measured.

"Let them go?" Carter snaps. "They've seen us. We can't let them go."

"It doesn't matter. Y—we can't just keep them here."

"You heard her. She's crazy. She's not going to keep her mouth shut. Neither of them are."

"Then what's your plan?" Julian's voice is exasperated, the question practically rhetorical, as if no feasible plan could ever exist.

There's a beat of silence, and then, "We have to get rid of them."

I press my ear harder against the door, straining to hear Julian's response. But instead, there's just nothing. I start to wonder whether they've left or are whispering, when he finally answers.

"What?" It's hollow, empty.

"Do you want the rest of your life ruined?" Carter snaps. He's angry, close to breaking.

"What are you talking about? What does 'get rid of' mean, Carter?" Julian demands.

"If those girls identify us, our lives, our careers, anything we hoped of having, is done. Over. They're nothing but a threat."

Another long silence ensues, and I'm beginning to doubt whether the conversation is still going to happen. Maybe Carter will kick the door open right now and kill me for eavesdropping. I wonder if they know I can hear them. Honestly, if Carter plans on killing us, he probably doesn't even care.

"You kidnapped her," Julian finally says. So quietly I almost don't hear him. But what I do hear is the weight behind his words. You kidnapped her. You hurt her. You took it too far. *You* did this.

After a beat, Carter answers, "I'm not going to let some bitch and her friend ruin my life. Are you?"

"No," Julian says, his voice back to normal. His tone is loud, clear. "You're right."

I pull back from the door as if I've been burned. I turn to Brooklyn, and while I know she couldn't hear the conversation, I feel like she can read it in my eyes. It's now or never. Shit just got real.

They're going to kill us.

Chapter 27

Silence ensues. For a long, long time. I'm not sure where the guys went. They're obviously no longer in the medical lab. I bang on the door a few times, wrestling with the handle, hoping to somehow dislodge the chair I know is propped up against the door, keeping us locked inside. But nothing works.

Eventually I turn back to Brooklyn and then scan the small room. "We need a weapon. Something to defend ourselves," I state. She nods. But there's nothing here. Nothing except . . . the drawers.

She realizes the same thing I do. She grimaces. "You don't think there'd be anything useful in there?" she asks.

I scrunch up my nose. "Probably not." I mean, they wouldn't keep tools in there with the cadavers, would they? But at the same time, I almost have to look. I have to. Because on the off chance that there's something in one of these drawers that saves our lives, it's worth the slightly scarring experience of looking past a dead body to get it.

I take in a deep breath, knowing that I'm the one to do it. Brooklyn won't. And I won't make her. She's been through enough.

But just as I'm about to take the first dive, explore the first drawer, the door bursts open behind us.

I twirl, and Brooklyn scrambles backward. Carter stands in the doorway, Julian behind him. In his hand he holds some sort of cloth—a rag? I recognize it as similar to what he held over Brooklyn's mouth in the dashcam footage. What had she called it earlier when recounting her story? Chloroform. Carter had told her it was chloroform. Wherever the hell you get that, I don't know. But I suppose however they plan on killing us, they'd rather we be unconscious for it.

Cowards.

Julian blocks the doorway while Carter takes a step forward. The area is small, so his step brings him halfway into the room. And then he lunges. I stumble backward, blocking Brooklyn, shielding her in the corner. But Carter keeps coming, and there's nowhere to go. His arm is outstretched, Julian behind him, ready to help with the struggle. I'm backed up to Brooklyn, who's already back against the far wall.

And before I can think to do anything else, before Carter can truly get to me, I reach for the drawer beside me and pull.

Groaning, it slides out like a file cabinet, right between us, the contents skidding to a halt at how suddenly I yanked it open—a body covered in a sheet, an arm visible, cut open, veins exposed, the skin and muscles white, pasty, like a plastic doll.

Everyone in the rooms screams. Me, Brooklyn,

Carter, even Julian. Carter trips backward, away from the body. I grab Brooklyn's arm and we duck underneath the drawer, making a break for the open doorway.

But while I make it, Brooklyn's arm is yanked from my grasp along the way. I turn back to see Carter pulling her against him, the cloth in his hand, while she struggles for dear life.

"Brooklyn!" I scream, and am just about to attack Carter with all I have when Julian beats me to it.

I stop, shocked. Julian grasps Carter's arm, yanking the rag from his hand and tossing it to the ground.

"What the fuck, man?" Carter bellows, distracted long enough for Brooklyn to break free of his hold. And with her gone, all his rage is now directed at Julian. He jumps at him, pushing him back until he crashes against the wall of drawers. The rattle echoes throughout the room. "I knew you were a pathetic piece of shit," he spits, his hands finding their way around Julian's throat. "I knew you didn't have the balls to do what it takes." His grip tightens while Julian claws at his hands, his arms.

"Go," I tell Brooklyn, pushing her toward the door. "Find a phone, call the police." She doesn't waste a second, and is immediately out the door and gone.

I turn back to Carter and Julian, aware that I have no weapon, but also aware that if I can just get him off of Julian, then maybe the both of us have a fighting chance against him. If Julian is truly turning against him. I'm just about to helplessly smack him on the back of the head with all I've got, when I notice the glint of something in his back pocket.

A scalpel. The knife he'd been holding to Brooklyn's throat when we first found them. I reach for it, pulling it from his pants, threatening, "Carter, let him go." But Julian's face is starting to turn blue, his arms are weakening. "Carter!" I shriek, body slamming him with my shoulder, doing anything I can to dislodge him.

And it works. Only now, he's turning on me. But as he turns, his grip leaving Julian's throat and now aiming for mine, I don't wait for him to land his target. I thrust my arm out, aimlessly, eyes closed tight, shrinking away from Carter's attack. The scalpel collides with something soft, yet hard.

And then there's a scream.

Only Carter doesn't stop. His hands reach my neck, his momentum pushing me backward. And with my last bit of strength, the last bit of grip I still hold on the scalpel, I twist. Hard. Again and again and again.

Carter makes some inhuman sound, finally twirling away from me, his attention on nothing but his own injury. A large, bloody, gash in his upper thigh. He sinks to his knees, clutching his leg that's turning a dark, dark red through his jeans. I stumble back, almost into the cadaver on the drawer behind me.

My gaze meets Julian's over Carter's crumpled form, a question in both our eyes. I think he's wondering if I trust him. After the last few hours of playing Carter's sidekick. And I'm asking if it was truly nothing more than playing. But the answer is settling over me as I take in the true innocence of his face—the hurt. The worry that I might actually never be able to forgive him.

I shoot him a weak smile. More of a grimace. But it seems to assure him all the same.

My attention slides back to Carter—to the massive amount of blood pooling around him. "Um," I start, beginning to feel sick at the sight of it. It's . . . a lot of blood. And Carter isn't even looking at us. Doesn't even seem mad. He's just rocking back and forth, his hands pressed to the wound in his thigh.

"Isn't there, like, an artery in your leg or something?" I ask, thinking back to my human biology class in high school. "I'm pretty sure there is."

"Yeah," Julian says weakly. As if suddenly snapped out of a stupor, he steps toward Carter. "We should get him out of the cold room." He hooks his arms underneath Carter's, who thrashes against him.

"Fuck off, man!" he snaps. "Fuck you."

"Carter," I say firmly, leaning down to try and subdue his flailing arms—surprisingly easy considering his former strength and rage. His eyes are glassy when they meet mine. "You're going to bleed out. We're just moving you."

Julian takes the moment of distraction to slide Carter the five feet out of the cold room and back into the medical lab. I close the door, shutting off the chilly breeze. The movement has caused Carter to let go of his leg momentarily, and I catch a glimpse of the wound. His jeans are torn from the scalpel, and the gash looks deeper than I thought it was. His entire pant leg is soaked now. And God, there's so much fucking blood.

I grimace, starting to feel worried. Julian shrugs off his jacket, kneeling beside Carter and wrapping it tightly around his thigh. Carter cries out in pain and angrily tries to swipe Julian away, albeit halfheartedly—either that, or he's really losing strength.

I sit back on my knees, watching Julian tie the jacket as tightly as he can. He looks up, and our gazes meet. Slowly, he straightens, watching me the whole time. Carter is breathing heavily between us, utterly focused on his pain.

"I thought he was going to kill her," Julian says quietly. "Pretending to help him was the only thing I could think of to distract him. To get the knife away from her so we could . . . think. Figure something out."

"So, you really *didn't* know," I say, but it's a statement waiting for assurance.

He leans forward, as if to reach for my hand, but realizes that Carter's blood-stained leg is kind of in the way. His eyebrows scrunch, and he seems momentarily distracted by the bleeding-out human being lying on the linoleum floor. But then he continues. "Everything I've ever said to you was the complete truth. I didn't suspect Carter until moments before you found Brooklyn's keys. I swear."

And maybe it's the sincerity in his eyes, the blood all over his clothes, the fact that he really did tackle Carter to the ground, or just my heart wanting desperately to believe him—but I do.

"Vally?" The door to the hallway opens, and Brooklyn peers in, a cellphone to her ear. She must have found either hers or mine. Her gaze darts to Carter's form, and her eyes widen.

"We'll probably need an ambulance too," she says softly.

Chapter 28

Julian and I sit, side by side, covered in Carter's blood. It itches, caked on my bare arms. The few police offers wandering around the station keep throwing us odd glances. Shock, concern, wariness. I suppose two bloody college students are not an everyday occurrence. But serves them right for ignoring my pleas about Brooklyn.

We've already been interviewed individually. I explained everything that happened—from Brooklyn's disappearance on Sunday to the disaster in the science building. And I suppose Julian told them pretty much the same story.

And now we've been sitting next to each other in silence, waiting. For what, I'm not sure. I guess for the clear to go home?

Carter and Brooklyn were both sent to the hospital—Carter to the ER and Brooklyn to be checked out after spending the last five days as a kidnapping victim. I'm assuming they'll both be interviewed as well. I called Sylvie and asked her to meet Brooklyn at the hospital so she'd at least have someone with her. Sylvie blubbered something about it being a miracle and promised to text me any relevant updates.

All I really want is to take a shower. And scrub the last five days from my entire existence. I'm not even sure what time it is. We've been at the police station for hours.

Part of me wants to speak. To say anything. But after the rollercoaster of a week we've had, Julian feels a million miles away from me—not merely a few inches. And he must feel the same, because he hasn't said a word to me since we arrived.

I keep opening my mouth, willing something to come out, but eventually, Julian beats me to it.

"I've had a crush on you since freshman year," he suddenly states, breaking the silence.

Without turning to look at him, I glance over, at his hands in his lap. He's gripping his knees tightly, tense. What an odd thing to say. Now, of all moments. And how strange that I'd had the exact same feeling.

"I always wondered if you noticed me. I always hoped we'd run into each other, that we'd have some reason to speak—to say hello, to comment on the weather, other people, anything," he goes on.

I think of all the times I'd arrive to class early, knowing Julian would be there too. I'd smile weakly at him and go sit at my desk in the back. Monday, Wednesday, Friday, we'd spend five minutes alone, in silence, waiting for the other to speak.

"I'd daydream about the day I'd finally have the courage to talk to you."

I turn to him now, almost angry. Because why didn't he? Because if only he'd said *anything*, I would have fallen at his feet. He could have declared the earth flat, and I'd agree with him.

"And then I did . . . only I can't imagine a way that this situation could have been more fucked up."

I'm staring at him now, only he won't look at me. It's true, I guess. His roommate kidnapped mine. What's worse than this?

And now *I* look back at all my daydreams. Of Julian smiling at me across the classroom, of us going on a study date, of him finally asking me out. I never thought, in actuality, that we'd end up sitting in a police station covered in his roommate's blood, finally spilling our feelings.

"I had a crush on you too," I admit.

This shocks him enough to finally look up.

I reach for his hand, clasping it in mine. "And I think Carter's the one who fucked it up. Not you. Not me."

The worry in his expression melts into something much softer. A mixture of things, maybe. Sadness, joy, hope.

An officer walks into the room, tearing our attention away from each other. "You're both free to go," he says. "We might call you in later with more questions, but for now, our focus is on Carter Williams."

We both mumble our thanks and goodbyes,

making our way outside into the darkened parking lot. I keep checking my phone, waiting for an update on Brooklyn.

We stop at the back of my car, the streetlight washing out Julian's complexion. His eyes look somehow darker.

There's a beat, and then, "I'm sorry." His voice comes out soft, broken. And while I've been incapable of trust for a long, long time—friends, people, especially men—there's a tiny little piece of me that cracks.

Closing the space between us, I grasp his bloodied shirt between my fingers and pull. And I kiss him.

There's no moment of shock, no moment of hesitation—just his lips meeting mine as if he'd been waiting for this all night. All week. All of our college career. And suddenly the only thing going through my head is the fact that I'm currently kissing Julian Sun. The boy I've had a stupid crush on since freshman year. The boy I prayed would notice me during class, on campus, in the lobby of our building. The boy who is now cupping my face, one of his hands sliding back and twisting in my hair, and kissing me like our lives depend on it.

His hands leave my face, and he's pulling me closer. Impossibly close. There's barely room to breathe. But who needs breathing anyway? Breathing is overrated. This. This is better than breathing.

I run my hand down his chest, and I can feel his

heartbeat beneath my palm. Fast. Like mine.

It isn't until minutes later that I finally pull away, still wrapped up in his arms, crushed against his chest, staring into dark, dark eyes that look just as surprised as mine probably do.

"You kissed me," he breathes, the ghost of a smile tugging at the corner of his mouth.

"Yeah. You kissed me too." I step back, and Julian's arms slide from my waist to my hands.

My phone lights up from my jacket pocket, and I pull it out to see a text from Sylvie. Brooklyn's okay. She's being kept overnight just in case. I glance back up to Julian. "I think after I shower, I'm going to try and visit Brooklyn at the hospital," I say. I don't know why I feel the need to tell him. I suppose after five days of being a team, it feels odd not to fill him in.

"Can I come?" he asks. "I mean, if she's okay with that—I don't know."

I nod. "Yeah, you can come," I agree, strangely relieved that he wants to.

I stare down at our two hands intertwined.

"I think I'm gonna move out. Find a new roommate," Julian states. There's a lot that needs to be said, and I'm glad he's, one by one, saying them all. "And you might need a new hobby."

I snort, and it turns into a laugh. "Yeah, that might be best."

Other Books by This Author:

Chapter 1

My coffee tastes like dirt.

I'm not really sure if that's a good thing or a bad thing. I mean, isn't coffee kinda supposed to taste like dirt? Or only a special, specific kind of dirt that only coffee experts are able to detect?

"How's your coffee?" Martin asks from across the table.

"Good."

"You know, this acidic flavor actually means the coffee beans have been roasted longer."

"Hmmm." I widen my eyes and do that weird smile thing that we've all done that isn't really a smile, but more of an acknowledgment of someone's existence or something they've said or done.

And why is everyone suddenly a coffee expert now? Aren't we allowed to know absolutely nothing about anything anymore? Why do we have to be experts? Actually, it's impossible to be an expert in *everything*, and yet that's what everyone is now. In fact, I'm going to now dedicate myself to knowing as little about coffee as humanly possible. I will ask the experts. I will seek their advice. My coffee-consuming experience from now on is in the hands of others. If only to eliminate the stink of "coffee snob" that's so elegantly floating around the small, preppy coffee shop we're currently sitting in.

There are empty burlap coffee sacks lining the walls. I didn't even know coffee came in that kind of bag anymore. Those old, fancily printed burlap sacks with countries like "Guatemala," "Kenya," or "Costa Rica" adorning the sides. I wonder how much money they spent on those "authentic" coffee sacks in order to staple them all over the walls so they could look like a cute indie coffee shop that cost exactly $10 to open and is run on nothing but laughter and happiness.

Martin suddenly looks uncomfortable at the lag in conversation. I ask him about movies and TV shows, which I realize is the most awful, cliché thing to ask. And I even hate being asked those questions myself. But isn't this what first dates are for? It's like New Person 101. What are the basics? The base-level intricacies of your humanity?

And I feel kinda bad because Martin looks nervous. Really nervous. And I hate when other people are nervous because then I get nervous.

Martin rattles off his list of favorite movies, which all happen to be in the Marvel Universe, or is it DC? I don't really know, because I don't really care about superheroes.

"So . . . what do you like to read?" he asks.

I squint a little, shrugging my shoulders, thinking up some sort of answer. I honestly hate this question. I'm not even sure why. I mean, I do read quite a lot. I like reading. It's the obvious follow-up question. And I can't blame him for asking it. I just asked him what his favorite movies are. But it's also kind of boring. Like, what does it really tell you if I love reading mystery novels, or I'm one of those snobs that only reads "the classics," whatever the hell those are? And what does it tell me if Martin loves superhero movies?

I already knew all of James's favorite books. The types of things he liked to read. The things I knew he'd hate. Sometimes I'd buy him one of those as a gag gift—*15 Steps to a Better Love Life*, or something equally as didactic. Only, I suppose if he'd actually read a book like that, we'd still be together.

And I wouldn't be sitting here. Trying to figure out what genre of book doesn't label me as either some kind of narcissistic elitist, or a child with no taste in literature.

"Uh . . . mystery books are fun."

And what does that say about me, you might ask? *Up for adventure, loves surprises, seems like a sweetheart, but has a mysterious air about her.* Probably has the same accuracy rating as my horoscope. I mean, I'm an Aquarius and they say we're supposed to be lucky in love, but holy shit is that wrong.

He smiles. "How fun. But don't you get tired of them? You know, all mystery books typically follow the same, basic formula."

And superhero movies don't?

"Uh . . . well, I mean, it's just for fun . . ." I stutter. Does everything have to be analyzed? Are we not allowed to just like something?

"Well, don't you want the media you're consuming to have some sort of depth to it?" He takes a sip of his acidic-meaning-it's-been-roasted-longer coffee and folds his hands in front of himself on the table.

I feel bad, but I'm really not in the mood for this. James would've poured his Folgers coffee into a shitty mug and gone with me to a used bookstore where we would've searched for the most ridiculous-looking sci-fi covers and bought those books for fifty cents each, not drilled me on the meaning of each and every aspect of the entertainment I enjoy and whether or not it *meant* something.

Stupid James.

"I guess I think that some things are just for fun. And that's okay. They don't always have to have . . . depth," I answer.

"Interesting." He doesn't actually seem interested. "But, on another level, doesn't everything have some level of depth to it? And we choose what we surround ourselves with, what we consume, what we put into our minds, so shouldn't we be more careful? Picky? Our time here on Earth is so limited. The things we experience should be nothing short of excellent."

Okay.

I sit there for a moment, staring at him, trying to figure out what the hell his endgame is here. Is this seriously a wooing tactic? Or does he just not like me?

"I'm sorry . . . are you saying I shouldn't read mystery books?" Is that your point? Did I get it? Or are you just trying to sound existential within the first half hour of our meeting?

"Not necessarily. I think the genre as a whole doesn't have much merit, but there are definitely some exceptions. Agatha Christie, for example. But, of course, she practically created the genre, and most things written after her were just a copy of what she did in the first place."

I pause for a moment. "So, other than Agatha Christie, I should probably just avoid the mystery genre?" I ask.

"Probably." He nods and purses his lips.

"Hmm."

I try and wait a somewhat respectable amount time before finding a way out of this tragically awkward excuse for a date.

"Martin, thank you for the coffee," I start.

"Marvin."

"Oh." Shit. "Sorry." I mean, what can I say? He introduced himself an hour ago, and the music was loud. It sounded like Martin. Which is honestly better than Marvin . . . but whatever, it's not like we're going to hang out again. "Thank you for the coffee," I say again. "I need to get going."

"Oh, okay." He looks slightly bummed, which I don't really understand, because it's not like we hit it off or anything. I'd have assumed he's just as eager to head home as I am. "It was nice talking with you."

I stand up. And here it is. The detestable will-you-hug-me, will-you-kiss-me (please don't), will-you-ask-me-out-again dance.

"We should hang out again sometime," he says.

I do that pursed-lipped-smile thing again, while standing just far enough away so that he won't lean in for the hug. "Yeah, I'll let you know."

Was that passive aggressive? Not too committal, but not too noncommittal.

We do another round of weird smiles, and then I head for the door. I beeline for my car and just sit there in the silence for a moment, locking my doors.

Well, my first date since James was . . . awful.

I mean, not awful. Just not good. I don't even know why I wanted this. Was having a boyfriend that great anyway? Why would I want another one?

To go to bookstores with, to go to dinner with, to go on hikes with, to bring you coffee, to buy you flowers . . . to cheat on you with his ex-girlfriend.

"Screw you, James," I mutter, starting my car.

Chapter 2

"I'm never going on a date again."

Amelia glances up from her lofted bed as I slam the door and chuck my keys on my desk in our cramped, low-lit dorm room. It's the kind of crappy, little room that most college students have experienced. We've strung Christmas lights along the walls and almost never use the overhead florescent light that Amelia claims "sucks the life out of her."

Criminal Minds is playing on the tiny TV that Amelia brought from home, and she's also halfway through a sudoku book—she's seen every episode at least twice, so she's resorted to multitasking through the show. We've been roommates for approximately one year and one month, and from the start, we were tied at the hip. It's amazing what mutual stress can do to people. We've confessed pretty much all of our deepest secrets and insecurities to each other over long nights of studying for tests we were certain we'd fail. Altmar University requires students to live on campus for two full years, so here we are again in Cowles Hall, ready to take our sophomore year by storm.

"I've decided that I'm going to die alone. And it's fine. Because the perfect guy doesn't exist. He just doesn't." I flop down on my bed, across from Amelia's. We've placed them parallel, across the room from each other, leaving space for our desks and dressers on the other end. "I mean, I thought he did. There he was. And then he cheated on me, proving that he's not a perfect man, and that all men are, in fact, awful."

"Not all men are awful," Amelia protests, half-heartedly continuing her sudoku from her bed.

"Yes they are."

She pointedly slaps her book against a pillow. "*Miles* isn't awful."

I smirk. "Okay, fine. You managed to find the *one man on Earth* who isn't a douchebag." Miles and Amelia have been apparently inseparable since freshman year of high school. They applied to colleges together, determined to go to the same one. And from the moment I met them, it was easy to see that they're deep in that ooey-gooey type of love. It would almost be annoying if they weren't such nice people. Miles even offered to change my tire the first week of classes when I ran over a nail in the campus parking lot. "Congratulations."

"Thank you." Amelia rolls her eyes. "Come on, Georgie. There are nice guys out there, you just don't want to see it right now. Not that I blame you."

I kick my shoes off and shoot her a mock glare. "What do you mean? I'm out there, I'm *trying*."

She finally gives up on her sudoku, dog-earing a page and setting it down. "You might feel like you're trying, but I think you're just mad right now. And for good reason," she adds quickly upon seeing my reaction. "But not all guys are like James."

James. Beautiful, intelligent, funny, selfish, horrible James. God, I'd really thought he was the one. We met at the beginning of our senior year of high school, sitting next to each other in our trig class. We bonded over our mutual hatred of the type of math that has no practical application, and after a month of flirting, he asked me out for coffee. And he was perfect. He was so stupidly, irritatingly perfect until he fucked it up.

It was halfway into our freshman year of college when he called. When he told me he wanted a clean break, a chance to get a fresh start, a new life. And that I should have the same. A college experience without a boyfriend weighing me down. A new life that was now tainted with anger, despair, and . . . no James.

It wasn't until a few months later that I learned the truth. That an ex of his had ended up at the same college as him, and one thing led to another and . . . he'd cheated.

But not all guys are like James.

I know Amelia's right, and I know I'm being unreasonable and crazy, but I really don't want to admit it. I groan and bury my face in my hands.

"I mean, blind dates are always kinda a risk," Amelia goes on, shrugging.

I nod, my face still obscured by my fingers. I was set up with Martin—oops, *Marvin*—by a coworker who thought we'd hit it off. Which probably means we're the only two single people she knows and therefore should automatically fall madly in love.

It's tough dating in the city of Newburg. It's just hard to find people. Although I suppose people say that about every city. Every town. Everywhere. It's just tough dating. Period.

"You could try online dating. You know, I have this friend from high school who met her current boyfriend that way."

I shake my head, finally freeing it from my grasp and letting my hands fall to my lap. "It just seems kinda creepy and . . . contrived."

Amelia shrugs. "Just an idea."

"Yeah."

I catch a glimpse of some mangled corpse on the TV screen and crinkle my nose. "You know, I might just be one of those people who never meets someone." I can feel myself spiraling. Doing that pathetic, woe-is-me dance, and I hate it, but here I am. Logically, I know it's ridiculous. It's like watching reruns of *The Bachelor* and seeing those contestants going home, crying in the van, lamenting how they're the only person in the world who'll never find love, and you just shake your head and think *nah, girl, you'll find someone; you're just being dramatic*.

But what if *I* am that person?

Amelia rolls her eyes. An expression that means *nah, girl, you're just being dramatic*.

"Seriously. Some people never meet anyone. That person probably didn't." I point to the twenty-something-year-old dead girl on the screen that Detective Gideon is so aptly inspecting.

"That person is fictional. That person got up and went home after filming. Probably to their significant other." Amelia adjusts her messy bun. Not a cute messy bun, but the kind you throw your hair up into once you're home for the day, the kind you'd never be caught dead in because it sticks up straight into the heavens and bounces around like it's its own entity.

I shoot her a look.

She softens her approach. "Besides James, your other boyfriends were nice, right? There are good people out there. You'll find one again."

I frown because I know she's right. James was a jerk. But Peter was a sweetheart. My boyfriend from freshman year of high school. He would buy me stupid, cute little gifts, and he taught me how to make out in the backseat of his car. But it was just one of those relationships you outgrew. For frustrating reasons that don't make sense, but are undeniably unignorable. And then my string of one-month will-we-or-won't-we romances up until I met James. The awkward getting to know you stage over and over and over again until I thought my brain would explode. And with every guy there was just something wrong, or something missing, or something that didn't click, and it was horrible and disheartening and exhausting.

"I hate dating," I say quietly.

Amelia shoots me an *I'm sorry* smile and slides off her bed. "Miles and I were gonna go get froyo. You wanna come?" She slips into her Birkenstocks.

It's sweet that they invite me to things that should probably be more of a date night activity. And sometimes I feel guilty for tagging along, but honestly, right now, froyo sounds amazing.

I wrangle myself back into my sneakers and grab my purse on our way out the door.

"Apparently Thursdays are their college student nights. Half price," Amelia is telling me as we head down the hallway. There are paper pineapples hanging from the ceiling and cardboard palm trees taped to the walls because this year's dorm theme is "tropical."

The girls live on the top two floors of Cowles Hall, and the boys live on the bottom. It seems to be pure luck that Amelia and Miles ended up in the same dorm. And pure luck that I happened to stumble upon such great friends.

The stairwell on the side of the building is the quickest way to Miles' room, and it echoes as Amelia's sandals slap down the stairs.

"I think they added bacon as a topping," I say. "Heather told me she noticed last week."

"Ew," Amelia laughs, and it bounces off the cement walls.

"Honestly though, bacon is one of those things that sounds gross on something, until you try it and then it's like—amazing." I shake my head.

We turn the corner, and I think it's Amelia who notices her first. What I notice is the smell. Iron. Thick and palpable. And then decay. I never knew bodies could smell so quickly. I always assumed it would take days. Apparently, it's only a few hours.

Amelia screams and it reverberates through the stairwell like a siren.

I don't say anything. I don't move. I'm frozen on the steps like someone is physically holding me there, unable to take my eyes off the girl at the bottom of the stairwell. Bent in a shape that no one's supposed to bend in, her eyes open. But that makes it worse. Because if they were closed, maybe she could be sleeping—unconscious.

Three mind-numbing seconds pass, and then a thought flits through my head.

Whitney. Her name was Whitney.

Acknowledgments

I want to offer a sincere thank you to everyone who helped me in the creation of this book.
Thank you to my editors from Pikko's House, Crystal Watanabe and Carla Pinilla.
Thank you to my cover designer, Mitxeran.
Thank you to my formatter, M. Dutchy.
Thanks to all my family and friends—the ones who send me pictures when they see my books in stores, the ones who ask me when my next ones are coming out, and the ones who patiently listen to all my ramblings and plot rants.
And once again, I feel the need to mention not only the mediocre men I've dated, but the worst ones too. If it weren't for you, I wouldn't have come up with this idea for a book.

About the Author

Polly Harris is the author of eight YA novels and runs her own editorial company where she works on books just like this one. When Polly isn't writing or editing, she can be found cuddling her cat (professionally known as her editorial assistant), crafting, or swiping through dating apps.

Hi!
Did you like the book?
Authors and their books depend on honest reviews to help them find readers!
I would love it if you took the time to write a review and it post on Amazon, Goodreads, or just email it straight to me. :)
harrispaulinec@gmail.com
paulineharriseditorial.com